WESTWARD TO FREEDOM

The New World Nautical Series
Book Three

David Field

SAPERE
BOOKS

WESTWARD TO FREEDOM

Published by Sapere Books.

24 Trafalgar Road, Ilkley, LS29 8HH,
United Kingdom

saperebooks.com

ISBN: 978-0-85495-090-4

'There's no discouragement shall make him once relent,
His first avowed intent, to be a pilgrim.'
John Bunyan, 1684

1

England, 1607

Long shafts of evening sunlight fell across the grass that Thomas Bailey was pretending to scythe. Since it was only early April it didn't require much scything, which was perhaps as well, since Thomas's eyes were fixed on the road that led to the manor house whose sloping front grass he was standing on. He missed his feet by inches as the blade swished harmlessly over its target.

As an indentured 'outdoor man' to local postmaster and bishop's bailiff William Brewster, it was Thomas's duty to challenge any strangers who wound their way up the dusty lane towards the manor house. He was not sure why, but he had his instructions. To further mask his true purpose, he was nominally supervising his master's seven-year-old daughter Patience, who would shortly be called inside by her mother to say her bedtime prayers. Playing alongside her was Mary Moore, the daughter of the Brewsters' steward, Matthew Moore.

One by one, the visitors sidled up the lane from the centre of Scrooby village, many of them casting furtive glances to the rear as they approached the manor house. Since Scrooby itself was on the Great North Road it was a regular resting place for those travelling between London and York, in which diocese it lay. The house now occupied by the Brewsters had once been dignified with the description of 'palace' when it had provided overnight sanctuary to Archbishops of York, of whom the best remembered was Cardinal Thomas Wolsey.

Had that revered prelate of the Church of Rome, now dead for almost a century, been advised of what was about to take place in his former palace, he would have demanded that those gathered for the purpose be excommunicated for blasphemy. But times had changed; the Catholic form of worship had been outlawed, and successive monarchs had taken the nation's religion down the road towards Lutheranism. However, it had not been taken as far as some would have wished, and those who were about to meet for worship in the manor house still risked persecution for their beliefs.

The new king, James, espoused religious freedom, but within limits. Those limits demanded the retention of a Church hierarchy over which he could preside as Defender of the Faith — an Episcopalian regime that made him doubly supreme. Not for him the emerging Puritan concept that God existed in the minds and hearts of all men, and that each church congregation should be independent, and outside any network of bishops and archbishops. During his youth in Scotland, James had seen firsthand the power wielded by Presbyterians who ran their own congregations, and the influence of charismatic troublemakers such as John Calvin and John Knox. The latter had been one of those calling for the execution of James's mother, Mary Stuart, the rightful Queen of Scotland.

So James was adamant that Separatist splinter groups of nominally adhering Protestants should not be allowed to thrive, for they would deprive him of direct control of religious matters through the bishops he might appoint. To this end, he declined to amend the legislation of his predecessor Elizabeth that was entitled 'The Act Against Puritans', and authorised imprisonment for anyone who attended private religious services instead of the established Sunday observances of the Church of England. James also urged his spies to seek out church ministers who appeared to be advocating Puritan philosophies and deprive them of their benefices.

Though such ministers were thrown out of their churches, this did nothing to lessen their influence among those who shared their more primitive views on how God was to be worshipped, and some of them had acquired almost martyr status among their followers. One such had been Robert Browne, who had been arrested for preaching his beliefs, only to be released under the influence of Queen Elizabeth's Chief Minister William Cecil, to whom he was distantly related. Browne had exiled himself to the more free-thinking Protestant Netherlands, where he established what became known as the Brownist Movement.

There were now countless Brownist congregations that met and worshipped in secret in the homes of their wealthier adherents, of whom William Brewster was one. The Brownist congregation that was destined to assemble that evening under the watchful eye of Thomas Bailey with his scythe had its own pastor, Richard Clyfton. He had so far succeeded in preaching dissenting views from his pulpit in the nearby parish of All Saints, Babworth, without being ejected from office.

Clyfton had been waiting anxiously inside Brewster's private chapel for the arrival of a distinguished visitor, who was being guided to the meeting by his assistant, John Robinson, a local man who had been deprived of his living in Norwich, but not before he'd fallen under the spell of the prominent dissenter John Smyth. Robinson was a lifelong friend of William Brewster and was about to repay his friend's hospitality — for Brewster had taken him in, along with his wife and children — by bringing into his house and congregation one of the most influential Brownists in England.

Thomas turned quickly as he sensed movement behind him. He was immediately questioned by a nervous Richard Clyfton from the shadow of the eaves above the front door.

'You have not laid eyes on good John Robinson with our visitor?'

'No, Pastor Clyfton,' said Thomas. 'They should be here soon, since the coach was to be met by Master Robinson at the crossroads at around this hour. The weather seems set fair, and I hear tell that the road from Norwich is a smooth one.'

'And you have spied no strangers? No-one whose face you have not previously seen entering our meetings?'

'No, Pastor. The master was most insistent that I be doubly attentive to that this day.'

'Very well,' Clyfton replied as he took one final look down the road. 'Do keep a good lookout, while I report back to Master Brewster, who grows anxious for their arrival.'

A further few minutes elapsed, and the sun was sinking lower behind the church tower to the west, leaving Thomas in shadow, when a woman called gently from the house behind him. It was Mary Brewster, the master's wife.

'Patience, dearest child, it is time for your evening prayers. And Mary should accompany you inside, as the air grows chill, and her father requires that she not be left out here alone. Thank you for your kind attention to them both, Thomas.'

'It was a pleasure, as always, Mistress,' Thomas assured her. 'Miss Patience seems to have a more winning disposition with each day, and she brings great credit to her father and your good self.' He turned away as he heard the distant rumbling of coach wheels, and he squinted into the setting sun towards the village crossroads.

The coach came to a halt beside him, and the familiar face of John Robinson smiled out. Thomas put down his scythe and opened the door to allow Robinson to descend onto the end of the driveway, then turn to smile encouragingly at the man whose coach it presumably was.

The visitor was tall, with long, greying locks, and he was inclined to a stoop. He smiled uncertainly at Thomas, unsure whether or not he constituted his welcoming committee, but at that moment Richard Clyfton came bustling down the drive with his hand extended in greeting.

'Well met, Master Smyth. I trust that God smiled upon your journey here from your home? We are blessed to have you grace our humble meeting, and we are all gathered within. Thomas, the steward says that you are to keep vigil until it grows dark, then you may cease your duties for the day. But before that you must show the coachman to the kitchen, where Cook will feed him, and young Master Jonathan will shortly attend in order to show him his quarters.'

'Yes, Pastor,' Thomas replied with the hint of a bow as he stood to one side to allow the visitor to be escorted to the front door of the manor house, where William Brewster was waiting to usher him in. Then Thomas beckoned to the coachman. 'You may stable your horse in the building to the rear of this one, where you will also find the kitchen. I will wash your coach, should you so desire.'

'You are most civil and obliging,' the coachman replied with a smile as he began to turn the coach in a wide circle in order to urge the horse up the long driveway to the left of the manor house.

Thomas walked dutifully alongside it. 'You journeyed this day from Norwich?' he asked.

'Gainsborough only,' the coachman replied. 'My master has many friends there, including those of your own John Robinson. Since John's suspension from his living in Norwich, and my master's return from Holland, there has, in the Fenlands, been much persecution of those who hold our beliefs. It is my master's fervent hope that his clandestine congregation may be joined with yours in the more joyful worship of God in the appropriate manner.'

'You mistake me, while flattering me,' Thomas replied with a blush. 'In truth I am not admitted to the congregation that meets under Pastor Clyfton's guidance and my master's generosity. I am a mere indentured servant.'

'As was I also, once,' the coachman replied as he brought the coach to a halt and stepped down from the box seat, 'so there is no shame in that. It is the Christian duty of men such as ourselves to loyally serve those who are called to, and chosen for, God's service.'

'Amen to that,' Thomas replied with a smile. 'The master has been good to me since the untimely death of my father, and it is a privilege to serve him. I hope that I give satisfaction, but you will shortly discover that he chose wisely in the appointment of Sarah Blount, the cook. Do you wish for assistance with your master's bags?'

Inside the manor house there was a warm welcome for their visitor, as Brewster shook his hand firmly.

'Welcome, my dear friend in God. It has been too long since I had the privilege of hearing your inspired teaching from your pulpit across the county boundary.'

'And it will be long before you hear it again from a pulpit,' Smyth replied. 'My days in Lincoln were all too brief, before I felt it safer to cross the Channel. And, as events have transpired, it would seem that God guided my hand in that.'

'Yet you returned?' Brewster asked.

Smyth sighed. 'A most grievous dispute regarding baptism, of which we may speak after our worship. That and certain other matters on which I seek your good counsel. But we must not keep the congregation waiting any longer, I propose.'

They moved into the large rear room, dimly lit by candles and with the curtains drawn to conceal the activities that were to follow. Brewster introduced their distinguished guest to the all-male congregation of some twenty or so, and the service began with a rousing rendition of Psalm 43, led by Smyth himself in a wavering tenor voice that tended towards the falsetto and betrayed his encroaching years. It then fell silent, and all eyes turned to their visitor as he launched into the long-anticipated oration that came directly from the heart he opened to God as usual, rather than relying on any pre-prepared sermon based on a passage from the Good Book.

'Dear friends in God,' he began, 'as we sang that most revered of psalms in the version most favoured by the inspiration for our form of worship, John Calvin, I am reminded also of a verse from Psalm 91, with which he also blessed us with his commentary and guidance. It contains the line "He that dwelleth in the secret place of the most High shall abide under the shadow of the Almighty."

'Are we not met in secret this night? Are we not forbidden to declare God's truth by those who seek to hide it from others, in order that they may preside unjustly over our worship in thrall to the sin of Pride? This house is surely "the secret place of the most High" that is spoken of in the Holy word, and we therefore bask in the certainty that we abide under the shadow of the Almighty.

'I bring you words of comfort from your friends under that same shadow. For you are not alone, and God sees your allegiance to His true word. The many secret places of the most High shall one day rise together to shout the truth of God's deliverance from the highest rooftops. For the day is coming, my good friends and neighbours, when we shall no longer need to meet like this, in secret, as did those early Christians who had witnessed the vile crucifixion of God's only son. Like them, we shall one day walk forward into the open light and proclaim the wondrous truth of God's redeeming power. Of His enduring love and mercy to those who have followed His path these many tormented years. Keep the faith, neighbours, and ours shall one day be the great glory, as we ascend to His holy place to receive our eternal reward. Praise be.'

'Praise be,' echoed twenty fervent voices, and it was left to Pastor Clyfton to pronounce the Departure Blessing following the rendition of two more psalms. Then the congregation moved through the house, and out into the pale light of the rising moon in deliberately small groups, lest there should be those watching the house in order to report the meeting to those charged with sniffing out Separatists, or Recusants as they were still called by some.

Brewster shook Smyth's hand warmly as the last of them sidled out with thanks and whispered blessings to their visitor. 'God speaks through you still, Master Smyth,' he said in tones of fervour inspired by the brief but most timely extempore address. 'Now, let us repair to the dining room, where we may break bread and partake of my good lady's parsnip wine.'

After an ample but plain supper, Brewster brought up one of Smyth's earlier comments. 'You spoke earlier of a certain sadness that accompanied your return from the Low Countries.'

Smyth nodded and put down his goblet. 'Indeed yes, and it may yet prove the undoing of that worthy congregation that saw fit to reject my exhortations on the matter of baptism.'

'The Church out there is split, say you?' Clyfton asked from further down the table. 'If so, it is an ill wind.'

'It is not split,' Smyth assured him testily. 'Say rather that there are differences of inspiration regarding how — and, most significantly, *when* — the true converts should be baptised into God's true Church.'

'And what say you?' Clyfton challenged him.

Smyth looked slowly round the assembled company before launching into what, on a Sunday morning and delivered from a pulpit, might have passed for a sermon. 'As those who have heard me preach will be well aware, it is my belief that true worship comes from within each of us, and cannot consist simply of chanting words from the Scriptures. The Bible is the work of men — particularly this most recent of ones, written according to the dictates of a king who seeks only to rule over the Church as well as the nation. It cannot rank above that which comes into our mouths when we are inspired directly by the Holy Spirit, as were the Disciples at the Pentecost. If we accept that true adherence to the word of God comes from the heart after deep searching of one's soul, then how can we in all conscience baptise into the Church of God small infants that have yet to acquire the gift of speech, yet alone the power of reasoning? Does it therefore not follow that baptism into the bosom of God can only be granted to those who, as adults with the power of reason and reflection, have chosen that path?'

'There is wisdom in that,' Brewster conceded.

However, the pastor of his own congregation, Clyfton, clicked his tongue. 'How may we therefore be assured that our dear offspring can be preserved from the wicked hand of Satan? If they be not baptised, where is the protection from sin?'

'In the love of God, brought down upon them by our prayers to Him,' Smyth replied with a frown in Clyfton's direction. 'To conclude otherwise is to deny the descent of God's mercy through the prayers of mankind.'

'How were things when you left the Low Countries?' Brewster asked quickly, anxious to prevent a religious dispute between two men for whom he had the greatest respect.

Smyth shrugged. 'They were arguing much as we seem to be doing,' he replied. 'But that brings me to the most important reason for my journey here to Scrooby. I wish to join your congregation here with mine from Gainsborough, that we might find power in worship through strength in numbers.'

'But they are a day apart,' Clyfton objected.

'They are here in England, certainly,' said Smyth. 'But I have in mind something more fundamental.'

Brewster's eyebrows rose. 'The Low Countries?'

'Indeed. To be precise, Amsterdam, where there is a group of my fellow adherents already assembled, but small in number. A larger number of them originally came with me from London, and were grandly named the "Ancient Church". Sad to say, many of them have fallen by the wayside, seduced onto false paths by my former fellow in Christ Thomas Helwys, who stoutly maintains that all men should be free to follow their religion of choice. This has led a good number of them to slide from purity and God's grace in pursuit of material aggrandisement, and when I seek to exhort them back to the true ways, they simply quote the misguided preaching of Helwys. In short, there is a need to inject the congregation in Antwerp with the strength that comes from congregations such as ours, which together could number well over a hundred.'

'And which together could fall into the same heresy as their predecessors,' Clyfton argued. 'Better that we remain where we are, in our smaller cells of purity, than expose our weaker brethren to the temptations of both Mammon and false gospels.'

Brewster looked thoughtfully around the table. 'I have long felt some discomfort with my position here in Scrooby. By day I maintain not only a public service for His Majesty, but also an administrative function for the Archbishop of York, while by night I host a form of religion that is anathema to them both. If I am caught out in the latter, my fall from office in the former will be doubly harshly dealt with. Many of our brothers in God have experienced periods of imprisonment for their faith — how long before it becomes a matter for execution?'

'You fear to play the martyr?' Clyfton all but goaded him.

Brewster shook his head. 'I have no concern for myself, but for my good lady wife and my children. Jonathan is not yet of an age at which he could assume the duties of head of a household, and Patience and Fear are but children. And if our holy work here is exposed, many good men around the county will be put to ruin.'

'I must own that I fear the same for my wife Bridget,' Robinson admitted. 'She is from wealthy stock, and her brother farms much land to the west of here, at Greasley. Were I to be taken up for my religious practices, that land would be forfeit to the Crown, and what then would befall Bridget?'

'The early Christians faced much worse,' Clyfton countered as he rose to his feet. 'I wish to hear no more fearful talk such as this. My final word on this subject is that if we move our congregations to Amsterdam inspired only by fear, then it is not a good reason, and I will not lead my flock into it.'

'It is Christ's flock, is it not?' Smyth reminded him. 'Beware the sin of Pride, brother.'

'And beware the folly of leading so many of God's children down a false path,' Clyfton retorted as he threw his napkin down on the table and stalked from the room.

2

The following morning, while the sun was still light pink, Thomas set about washing the Smyth coach, as he had undertaken to do. Armed with a bucket from the well at the foot of the back garden, and an old shirt that he'd been keeping for just such an occasion, he began with the roof and worked his way down vigorously in an attempt to warm up the muscles that were feeling tight in the early morning chill.

There was a flash of blue smock from around the rear of the coach, and Amy Tasker the kitchen wench appeared. Her open, freckled face lit up with a smile as she handed Thomas a cob loaf that was still warm to the touch.

'Cook says you can have this, and could you cut her some more logs for the fire?'

'Tell her thank you, and that I'll cut them just as soon as I've finished this.'

'Why are you washing a visiting coach?' Amy asked, eager as ever for an excuse to tarry with the handsome, broad-shouldered nineteen-year-old with the deep brown eyes that made her head spin every time she stared into them.

'Because I promised I would,' he replied.

Amy adopted her most coquettish smile. 'So if you promise to take me to the summer fair in Bawtry, you'd feel obliged to keep that promise?'

'Yes,' Thomas smiled back at her, 'which is why I won't be making such a promise in the first place. The Good Lord alone knows what I'll be doing by the time the summer fair comes around.'

'We might all be over the sea somewhere,' Amy whispered conspiratorially. 'Cook has it from the steward that the master and his visitor sat up late into the night talking of going abroad somewhere. Will we all have to go with them, do you think?'

What she was really asking was whether or not she'd still have a home and a place in service by the end of the year. She'd been selected from a local poorhouse whose superintendent had assured William Brewster that she was the most hardworking young woman in the establishment, and she had no idea whether or not she might find a family that would take her in were her duties in the manor house kitchen to come to an end. Thomas knew of her orphan status; he knew also that she doted on him and would happily give herself to him in return for some sort of security, but he had never sought to take advantage of her. Instead, he thought of her as a vulnerable creature in need of care, much like a fledgling fallen from a nest. She was someone to whom he could relate, given the uncertain future that had opened up for both Thomas and his middle-aged mother when his father had died unexpectedly of a fever five years previously. He felt protective towards Amy, but nothing more, despite her less than subtle hints that something else might be available for the asking. Now he could understand her fear that the only life she knew might be taken from her.

'Surely, if the master moves away, he'll be taking us with him?' he said.

Amy shrugged. 'Who can tell? But if he takes you, will you take me along with you?'

'Won't that be a matter for the steward to decide?' Thomas replied evasively, just before a reedy but commanding voice interrupted their conversation.

'There you are, girl!' Jonathan Brewster called with his usual pomposity, his puffy fourteen-year-old face set in a look of haughty disdain. 'You're required in the kitchen, not out here feeding bread to another servant. As for you, Bailey, why is this coach only half washed? Pastor Smyth will be requiring it for his return to Gainsborough after breakfast, which will be long delayed if this maid tarries any longer, wasting her time with you. Off you go, girl!'

Amy scuttled away with a red face, and Thomas gritted his teeth as usual as he strove to speak civilly to his master's oldest child.

'It will, they say, be a late breakfast anyway, given that I hear tell that your father kept our guest talking until late into the night. Have no fear, Master Jonathan, this coach will be fully clean when the time comes for the departure.'

'See that it is, and guard your soul against the evil of fleshly temptations. Amy is but another that is sent into this world to tempt men from the narrow thorny road towards God's chosen kingdom. As for what my father's business may have been with our esteemed visitor, it is no concern of yours, and you should pay no heed to servant tittle-tattle. Continue with your duties.'

Thomas nodded and dipped the old rag back into his bucket. Tempting though it was to throw the contents of the bucket all over Master Jonathan, it would be a tiresome walk back to the well, and he'd been reminded that his job was only half complete. With a sigh, he turned his back on the master's son and walked round to the other side of the coach in order to begin work on the second half of its roof.

Having finished that, and eaten the last of his breakfast, he began cutting and splitting the logs that Cook required for her fires. He stacked them outside the kitchen, which, like most that had been constructed as part of a Tudor manor some years in the past, was located in the garden as a precaution in case it caught fire. He heard a cheery voice calling his name, and straightened up and turned as he saw young William Bradford heading his way. They were good friends, in the sense that they enjoyed each other's company on the many occasions when William would attend at the manor house to borrow a book from William Brewster.

Like Thomas, William Bradford was fatherless, but for him family bereavements had been more tragic and fundamental. Having lost his father in the first year of his life, William had been sent to live with grandparents on the remarriage of his mother. Their deaths had been followed by the death of his mother, leaving William an orphan by the age of seven, dependent on the charity of two uncles. He was now seventeen, with an impending moustache that sought to match his mop of unruly black hair.

Since the age of twelve William had been drawn to the preaching of Richard Clyfton, first in his parish church and more recently in the Brewster manor house. William was the youngest member of the secret Scrooby Separatist congregation, and one of its most ardent. But his own background as the orphaned son of modest farming folk had instilled in him an appreciation of honest toil, and he admired Thomas's open, if sometimes blunt, manner, and his loyalty to his master.

Thomas grinned as he looked at the book tucked under William's arm. 'Is there aught left in the master's library that you have not read?'

William laughed. 'Some are worthy of being read more than once, as you would discover if you took the trouble to read.'

Thomas never took offence at these regular references to his aversion to the written word, despite the excellent education he'd received at the local church school that his late father had diligently paid for, year after year. Thomas preferred action rather than words, and he had his own gentle way of dealing with William's gibes. 'You'd lose some of that puppy fat, were you to spend less time reading, and more time in exercise such as mine,' he teased. 'There are more logs to be cut, should you have a mind to do so.'

William chuckled. 'In truth I have more important calls upon my time, the foremost of which would seem to be the arranging of my few meagre possessions for travel. I trust that you will be accompanying us, for I would feel the loss were you not there to take me to task regarding my love of God's bounty from the land.'

'Accompanying you where?' Thomas asked uneasily.

William cocked his head. 'You really have not heard? Our humble congregation of some thirty or so are minded to move across the county boundary into Gainsborough, there to merge with the followers of Pastor Smyth.'

'Including the master?'

'*Led* by your master, or so he advises me. He is to resign his current offices and seek gainful employment of a similar nature in our new abode, so it is to be anticipated that his household will travel with him. He has not yet told you?'

'I get my daily orders from the steward,' Thomas explained, 'so I rarely speak to the master directly. The mistress, certainly, when she entrusts Mistress Patience to my supervision here in the garden, but not the master.'

'Well, perhaps the steward will have something to impart shortly,' William suggested. 'In the meantime, I must take my leave of you. Do not trouble yourself to leave me some logs to split.'

It was three days before Thomas received confirmation that his contented existence as the 'outside man' of Scrooby Manor was shortly to come to an end. The steward, Matthew Moore, called all the manor servants to a meeting in the kitchen, where they stood or sat, according to their own perceived hierarchy.

'The master has determined to move himself, together with his family and household, across the county border to Gainsborough, there to be closer to Pastor Smyth,' Moore announced. 'Others of his Christian fellowship will also be transferring with him, which will leave little work in this locality for any of you who choose to remain here.'

'Are you saying as how we can move with the master?' Sarah, the cook, asked nervously.

Moore nodded. 'It is his wish that the entire household shall transfer with him.'

Amy, standing next to Thomas, gripped his arm, leaned in and whispered in his ear, 'See? You can't shake me off that easily!'

Thomas smiled sideways at her as he reminded her that there had been talk of moving across the Channel, rather than just to Gainsborough. 'Then you won't be able to pursue me unless you can swim.'

Given the uncertain alternative, everyone currently in Brewster's service cheerfully agreed to move wherever the master took them, such was their respect for such a generous and God-fearing employer, but Thomas required a little more clarification before he could break the news to his widowed mother in her lonely cottage just down the road in Blyth. He waited until the following morning, when Moore came to him with instructions to cut more rushes from the banks of the nearby River Ryton and leave them by the back door for the housekeeper, then he took his opportunity.

'Shall we be venturing further afield than Gainsborough in due course?' he asked lightly.

The steward's face set in a frown. 'And what might have given you that idea?'

'Well, I had it from Amy in the kitchen, who had it from Cook, who claims to have had it from you, that the master and Pastor Smyth have in mind the possibility of crossing the water into the Low Countries. If that be the case, and if we are all to follow in the master's service, then I would wish to advise my elderly widowed mother that I may be gone further from her side for a while, and perhaps for a period of time that will see her natural lifespan come to an end.'

'You must say nothing to others of what you have heard, do you understand?' Moore glowered. 'If Cook spent more time ensuring that she gave good account of the money passed to the butcher, the fishmonger and the poulterer, and less time in idle gossip, then the manor accounts might be healthier.'

'So it is not true?' Thomas persevered.

Moore looked round carefully before lowering his voice. 'You may certainly inform your mother that you may be gone for some time, but you must make no mention of possible travel into Holland. It is of the utmost importance that you obey that instruction, do you understand? It is not safe, in these uncertain times, to voice abroad any suggestion that the master might be departing the realm. In order to be allowed to do so, he would need the king's authority through the hand of the County Commissioner of the Peace, who is not well disposed towards the master because he gave sanctuary to Master Robinson after he was ejected from his living in Norwich for his Recusant preachings.'

'I will exercise the discretion that you prescribe,' Thomas assured him, 'and you may rely upon me to keep silent regarding our ultimate destination.'

'It is Gainsborough and nowhere else, understood? Now, set about your duties and engage in less idle speculation.'

It was fortuitous that Thomas's duties for the day took him to the banks of the river, because he was able, by dint of working at double his normal speed, to load the estate wagon with rushes well before the sun was at its highest point in the early summer sky, then take it down the river path to Blyth, where his mother earned a precarious living as a washerwoman. She welcomed him home on his unexpected, and rare, visit, then sat him down and insisted that he partake of some potage and bread.

'Now then, why are you here?' she demanded in that way of hers that allowed no evasion. 'The Good Lord knows I see little enough of you, and that you only grant me a visit when you've something special to tell me, so what is it this time? Have you met a young woman and plan to marry? Or have you perhaps done more than just meet a young woman, and have to marry her quickly?'

'Neither, Mother,' Thomas replied with a blush. 'It is that my master will shortly be transferring to Gainsborough, and perhaps further afield, which will mean that my visits will be less frequent.'

'If they were any less frequent, I might forget that I even have a son,' his mother smiled, 'but you needn't concern yourself that I'll be left without a soul to see me through me declining years. I've had an offer of marriage from Edward Matthews, the miller, and I'm minded to accept it. Now that you're here, you can give it your blessing, then I'll be Mistress Matthews the next time you bless me with a visit.'

Thomas was overjoyed at the news, since he had worked for Matthews in his younger days, and had a high regard for the man. It also relieved him of any guilty conscience, and any concern he might have had for his mother's welfare while far away from her. He embraced her warmly, wished her God's blessings, and urged the horse back along the road to Scrooby with a lighter heart.

Thomas proved to be far from the only person interested to learn of Brewster's ultimate intentions after he formally resigned his two commissions on the grounds that he wished to transfer himself to Gainsborough in order to be closer to 'his old friend John Smyth'. For one thing, Smyth himself was under suspicion of being at the centre of a web of Separatist intrigue in Lincolnshire. Word had come back from royal spies in the Low Countries of his promotion of a new form of Calvinism calling itself Baptism, and of his need to return to England because of the split that his extreme views had caused in the English Calvinist community in Holland. There was also the fact that William Brewster had never been reported, by those who kept a watchful eye on his movements, as being a close associate of his so-called 'old friend' Smyth.

It was therefore a highly sceptical Commissioner of the Peace for the County of Nottinghamshire who called on Brewster one day at Scrooby Manor, and demanded to know the real reason for his resignation from office and his avowed intent of crossing the county boundary into Lincolnshire. It was also reported that others in the village were making preparations to leave, and it was suspected that Brewster was planning to set up a subversive cell of Recusants resistant to His Majesty's oft-expressed desire for an established Anglican Church over which he might preside.

'Be in no doubt, Master Brewster,' Commissioner Mitchell warned him with a sneer. 'You will be carefully watched wherever you go, and should you not attend Sunday worship as ordained by law, you will be taken in charge and severely questioned. The same is true for your household.'

'Rest assured that I am fully cognisant of what the law requires of me,' Brewster replied with a smile, 'and I will not delay your presence in my house any longer by seeking to debate what *God* requires of me.'

The commissioner departed, eager to report his attendance, and his lingering suspicions, to those who would ultimately convey them to His Majesty. Brewster passed the word to those who had undertaken to accompany him eastwards that they should be guarded in their affairs, and should, if possible, seek to make their departure seem like a mere holiday.

3

As the first of the early morning mists rose from the nearby fields to remind them that autumn was upon them, the village of Scrooby all but emptied as some thirty members of Clyfton's congregation, along with their families and servants, crossed the county border and arrived in Gainsborough in small enough clusters to make their departure seem innocent. Once they arrived, they learned that their inspirational pastor, Richard Clyfton, had not only been deprived of his incumbency in nearby Babworth, but had been expelled from the Church of England.

Many of those who had departed Scrooby did not entertain any realistic expectation of settling permanently in Gainsborough. Even though, to begin with, the two Separatist congregations met up either in Gainsborough's Old Hall, or in large country houses conveniently located deep in the Lincolnshire countryside, this was only for long enough for them to get to know their future fellow travellers to Holland.

While the rest of their party set about finding such accommodation and employment as they could, the Brewster family had been met on their arrival in Gainsborough by Richard Smyth, brother of the inspirational John, who advised them that John had already taken ship secretly to the Low Countries, along with a select few of his congregation. He had left word that the Brewster household were to be allowed to occupy his abandoned house and land, along with their servants, while they awaited their own passage out to join him.

The house to which they were taken, to the south of Gainsborough in a village called Lea, had been neglected. The

Brewster household gazed with shaking heads at the fallen roof timbers and sagging woodwork of the old house, and the dilapidated state of the old cow barn between it and the copse of trees that had once been a fine orchard. For the next few weeks, Thomas was kept constantly at work patching roofs, propping up doors, replacing panelling and conveying stacks of firewood indoors to keep the gathering winter at bay. Occasionally he would also catch rabbits for the pot, and to celebrate the first 'full worship' of the dispersed congregation that made the effort to travel to Lea, he even caught a sheep on neighbouring land at dead of night, slit its throat and presented the still warm carcass to a delighted Sarah Blount, the cook.

It was also during this period that John Robinson was formally ordained, at the hand of his nominal superior Richard Clyfton, as a second pastor in the Assembly of God, as the congregation was now known. Also rising to a respected position in this group was the still youthful William Bradford, whose seeming wisdom and spiritual grace belied his years, and set him apart as a sturdy soul who might confidently be expected to one day assume a greater role in the governance of the congregation.

In the third month of this existence, Thomas was carrying a pile of logs into the main room and stacking them by the fire early one evening when Amy met him in the passageway. She was carrying a sack and wearing a frown.

'I'll miss you while you're away, but here's something to keep you fed on your journey,' she pouted, then began to walk away.

Thomas called her back with a frown. 'What journey might that be?' he asked.

Amy tutted. 'There's no need for secrecy with me, Tom Bailey. It's no secret, anyroad, that you're to travel with the

30

master to Boston, wherever that might be. In this sack is a large manchet loaf and some dried fish. It'll last you for two days, then you'll need to get more from wherever it is you're going to.'

'Why does the master travel to Boston, and why does he require me to accompany him?'

'Ain't he told you?'

'Would I be asking, if he had?'

'Well, he clearly didn't confide in me,' Amy said self-consciously, 'nor even Cook, although as usual she had the ear of the steward, who'll be travelling with you. It's said as how the master's seeking a vessel to cross the sea to Holland. And the sooner the rest of us are rid of this place, the better — I'm sick and tired of chasing rats away from the bread oven.'

The following day, Thomas duly found himself instructed to don his best boots for travel and jump onto the front board of the open wagon that conveyed the three men first to Lincoln, and then on to Boston after an uncomfortable night in an inn that was safely off the main road, but had little else to recommend it. Once in Boston, they made their presence known to the sympathetic Separatist group that was well established and had already succeeded in smuggling abroad a sizeable number of Smyth's former Gainsborough congregation. They were guided by them to the waterfront, where they were told to enquire after a Captain Johannes van Gelder, who was the master of a vessel large enough to carry a hundred assorted passengers — men, women and children — down the North Sea and across to Antwerp.

They entered a noisy alehouse on the waterfront, where they met with van Gelder and agreed to assemble one week hence at a place called Fishtoft, where his vessel would be moored at Scotia Creek. From there, they would float downriver on the tide into the creek known as The Haven, which led out into the North Sea. Moore grudgingly handed over the agreed deposit, but he was still uneasy as they gratefully slipped away from the drunken cacophony in the sailors' favoured alehouse.

'How do we know we can trust him?' Moore demanded.

Brewster turned to him with a smile. 'It is not him in whom we trust, but God.'

Back in Gainsborough, there was a week of fevered activity, and much hiring and borrowing of wagons, as the group of nearly a hundred prepared for the next stage in their journey towards religious freedom. Thomas was placed in charge of loading the two wagons that contained all that was left of Scrooby Manor, including the staff. After an uncomfortable night under wagon canvas, they reached the outskirts of Boston, where they were directed through the town and out onto the Fishtoft Road. The smell of seaweed and old fish grew stronger as the procession rumbled down the lane between waterways that were filling slowly with the incoming tide. As they rounded a bend the tall masts of a coastal barque came into sight from behind a copse of trees. Those in the first wagon gave a cheer, and the horses were urged forward.

Tired passengers were assisted down onto the dusty foreshore by family servants, the more elderly stretching aching limbs while others scurried into the trees to answer long overdue calls of nature. Captain van Gelder was nowhere in sight, but a gangplank had been lowered, and Brewster was urging his companions to mount it when there came a series of loud commands from the hedgerows on either side of them. Men armed with muskets surrounded them, and a tall man strode into the centre of the group. He was wearing a tricorn hat and brandishing a staff of office.

'I am Emerson Padley, Commissioner of the Peace for Lincolnshire, and you are all under arrest for suspected sedition and blasphemy. Take them to the waiting boats, men.'

4

The would-be escapees were marched further along the lane, round another bend in the stream, to a point where a long line of flat-bottomed boats had been tied up alongside a wooden pontoon. Once they were all assembled, Commissioner Padley stepped forward with a scroll of parchment in his hand.

'When these names are called, those to whom they belong shall step forward. William Brewster first.'

Brewster stepped forward, his wife Mary by his side, holding her infant daughter Fear close to her bosom. Their son Jonathan reluctantly took his little sister Patience by the hand, and after a moment's thought stepped forward as well. Padley frowned and waved them back with his free hand.

'I called only for William Brewster. The others must step back.'

Brewster looked helplessly behind him as his family members reluctantly did as ordered, and he caught sight of Thomas. 'Thomas, into your care I entrust those that are dearest to me,' he instructed.

Thomas walked forward to stand directly in front of the bewildered Brewsters. He felt a cold hand in his, and he turned to see Amy by his side.

'I'm kind of family as well, aren't I?' she smiled hopefully, and Thomas nodded.

'Richard Clyfton!' Padley called next. John Robinson and William Bradford followed soon after.

As the small group formed up in front of all those who had planned to be on board the vessel intended for Holland, it became obvious that whoever had supplied the list of names to the local official had been someone who knew the former Scrooby congregation well. Perhaps it had been one of their number who had stayed behind, Thomas thought. The company on the riverbank contained a few of the remaining Gainsborough Brownists who had not gone across to the Low Countries in the first wave, but none of them was commanded to step forward, so the list had to have come from Scrooby.

Those selected were ordered into the first of the flat-bottomed craft, and Padley turned from supervising their loading to shout an instruction to those who remained.

'The rest of you will be loaded into these remaining vessels, and you are all destined for the Boston Guildhall, there to answer for your disobedience to religious laws enacted by our most gracious Majesty, King James. You will all serve as a warning to those whose misguided beliefs and blasphemous practices might otherwise tempt them to disobey the laws of this realm. During your passage to Boston, the officers under my command will conduct necessary searches of your persons for hidden weapons or items of value, of which you will be deprived. Now, let us waste no more time.'

The remainder of the party began to form into natural groups. Thomas turned to face the Brewsters, whose safety he was now responsible for. Before he could say anything, Jonathan Brewster puffed out his cheeks and announced, 'In Father's absence, I'm obviously the head of the family, so follow me.'

He turned and began to walk down the riverbank to the nearest boat, dragging little Patience after him. She squealed and called out for her mother, and Mary Brewster looked apprehensively at Thomas, who smiled as he gestured for her to follow her son.

They climbed into the waiting craft behind Jonathan, while all around them others were being ordered to board other craft by the villainous-looking officers. The Brewster family and their companions, including Thomas and Amy, were ordered to sit in the scuppers of the shallow boat. From a platform to the rear, a muscular boatman pushed them out with a long pole, and thereafter kept dipping his pole into the silt of the river to enable them to make slow but steady progress down the creek to where they would meet the broader waters of the Haven, and could steer a course back upstream into Boston.

They had barely pushed off when the two officers who had been assigned to their vessel began searching their prisoners. They began mildly enough, insisting that everyone empty their pockets, and confiscating obvious items of modest jewellery, mostly of a religious nature, from necks and wrists. They also made a pile of the Bibles that most of the passengers had been carrying on simple belts or other attachments around their waists.

Then, as they met no resistance other than sullen stares, they became more ambitious, and insisted that their captives must be hiding more valuable items inside their clothing. This was the only excuse they needed to sexually abuse the few women on board, taking unnecessary time to fondle around their bodices, or probe beneath their gowns. The male prisoners who were with them looked on in silent fury, and Thomas was debating whether to challenge such brutality when one of their captors walked up to Amy with a leer, his hand extended towards her left breast. Amy gave a squeal of fear, and Thomas grabbed the man's wrist in a bear-like grip. The man looked at him apprehensively as he asked, 'She's your woman?'

Thomas nodded and relaxed his grip as he felt the man pulling his hand back. As the officer turned and walked further down the vessel, towards where the Brewster family were huddled, Amy planted a dry kiss on Thomas's cheek. 'I'll hold you to that,' she whispered gleefully.

Thomas saw where the officer was headed next and leapt to his feet. 'I don't think I'll be able to employ the same ruse this time, though, so "your man" may be about to get himself killed in the line of duty.'

He strode between the tangle of legs sprawled across the deck to where the officer was now confronting little Patience Brewster. Her eyes were wide with fear as the man reached for the hem of her gown, only to be warned off by a growl from Thomas.

'Hold your hand from that child!' he demanded.

The man turned, spat on the deck and glared up at Thomas. 'Is she your woman and all? She's just a tiny lass.'

'She's the daughter of my master, and I'm sworn to protect her, so if you proceed with what you had in mind, I'll wring your neck.'

'I'm armed with a club,' the man threatened.

'And I'm armed with a sense of what's right,' Thomas replied. 'So let's see which weapon is the stronger, shall we?'

The man turned away with a curse and picked his way back down the vessel, kicking any ankles that hindered his passage.

Jonathan Brewster finally stepped out from behind Patience with a haughty sneer. 'That wasn't strictly called for, since I was here,' he all but chastised Thomas.

'I suggest that you ask Mistress Patience how she valued that arrangement,' Thomas replied before walking back to Amy.

When they reached Boston, the prisoners were herded into the square in front of the Guildhall, and Commissioner Padley called out to the curious crowd that had gathered.

'Here be they that sought to leave our shores, in thrall to the Devil that they worship,' he announced. 'The magistrate awaits them, but you are invited to demonstrate your displeasure at their rejection of our godlier ways.'

By the time that the last of the fifty or so of the prisoners had been dragged before the town magistrate, many of them bore vegetable and fruit stains down the fronts of their tunics. The first inclination of the magistrate had been to release them upon payment of a bond, until several outraged prisoners explained to him that all their money had been taken by their captors. The magistrate frowned before advising all but four of them that they were free to go, after swearing an oath that they would present themselves on the days set for their trials on minor charges in his court.

The four who were not liberated were Brewster, Clyfton, Robinson and Bradford. They were advised that they would be held in the cells until bond money was forthcoming for their release on bail, since they were due for trial at the next quarter sessions at the end of the year. They would face charges for the violation of the Act that required all men to worship nowhere other than in their own parish churches.

By the time the rest of them wandered disconsolately back outside, it was growing dark, they had nowhere to go, and they were penniless and hungry. Thomas sat down heavily on a mounting block, wondering what they might all do next. He became conscious of a presence at his elbow and looked up at the solemn face of a man dressed for some sort of trade.

'You serve Master Brewster, do you not?'

'I have that privilege, certainly,' Thomas confirmed. 'To whom am I speaking?'

The man lowered his voice. 'My name is William Smyth, and I am a ship's chandler by trade. My father and uncle are known to you, and you were residing on my uncle's property before you sought to evade the authorities.'

Thomas nodded his understanding of what the man was trying to tell him without exposing himself to any trouble. The name of his uncle John Smyth had been high on the list of those sought by Commissioner Padley, but he was now presumed to be safely back in Holland with those of his flock who had succeeded in escaping. The father of this man had also risked prosecution by putting them all in contact with the treacherous Dutch sea captain.

'What are your immediate plans?' Smyth asked.

'Other than guarding my master's family, I have no plans,' said Thomas. 'We do not even have a roof over our heads this night.'

'Might you not return to my uncle's property in Lea, humble though it be?' Smyth asked. 'At least it almost has a roof once more, which I am advised is thanks to your skill with an axe and hammer.'

With no alternative, Thomas organised a small party of youths from among those who had just been released from the gaol to walk back to Fishtoft and retrieve the wagons that had been abandoned. He then led the Brewster family party back to the dilapidated property south of Gainsborough that they had left only days earlier with such high hopes. Most of their congregation followed them, having no better idea of what to do.

Back at the Smyth property they held a brief meeting, and Mary Brewster expressed her concern for the health of not only Patience, but also her two-year-old daughter Fear, if they were to face the cold, wet months ahead in the rudimentary shelter that had been just about bearable during autumn. Her son Jonathan agreed with her and nodded towards the ruin of the old house that John Smyth had once occupied.

'That's where the likes of us should be housed, in greater comfort than we have enjoyed hitherto. After all, we're lords of the manor.'

'We were, once,' said Mary, 'but now we're wandering souls, and the head of our family is in Boston Gaol.'

'Master Jonathan has a point, though,' said Sarah, the cook. 'At least there's a kitchen of sorts out the back there. I couldn't guarantee that I'd be able to keep feeding you all using the wood fires we burned outside when we were last here. If Master Thomas could put a new roof on the old kitchen, I'd be better placed to turn out wholesome food, assuming Master Thomas can find the ingredients.'

'While he's about it, he can restore more of the roof on the old house,' Jonathan added, 'then at least we can begin to enjoy the comfort to which we're entitled.'

Thomas sighed. 'Where do you want me to begin? Catching food for the pot, restoring the house roof, or rebuilding the kitchen?'

'You're the "outside man",' said Jonathan. 'So stay outside here and set about all the jobs we've given you. In my father's absence, I'm authorised to give you your orders.'

'Are you also authorised to assist me?' Thomas demanded.

Jonathan reluctantly agreed to undertake responsibility for finding food. 'After all,' he boasted, 'I'm the better shot.'

'And what were you thinking of using for ammunition?' Thomas asked. Jonathan had no answer, so Thomas went on, 'In the days before the musket came into use, our predecessors used things called spears and bows. If I make a few, and show you how to use them, can you undertake to be our provisions man?'

Jonathan agreed, and over the next few days he began to return triumphantly from the nearby copse with rabbits. Then he discovered that the estate pond was still supplied with lampreys and other fish, and for two weeks Sarah was tested to the limit, finding new and appetising ways to serve them with what few spices she could find in the abandoned pantry. Thomas concentrated on felling timber, which he used to rebuild the roof of the main house, where the Brewster family retired every night. Thomas, Amy, Sarah and a downcast Matthew Moore and his family once again occupied the former barn. On two occasions Thomas sneaked into the neighbouring fields, where he slit the throats of sheep that were too slow to outrun him. For a month or so, the family fed on mutton, until the remainder of the carcasses became too rotten to consume even when heavily spiced.

The community had not lost sight of the fact that their leaders were still being held in the narrow cells of Boston Gaol, awaiting trial. Before then, the rest of them would need to answer to their oaths and take what punishment awaited them, and the steward did his best to organise daily prayers to preserve their souls.

When the lesser accused, who included Thomas, were summoned to court for their transgression in 'foolishly following the lead of the Godless', Thomas pointed out, on behalf of the Brewster retainers, that they were in the main indentured servants bound by law to follow their master. Since the magistrates trying their cause had indentured servants of their own, they were not about to argue with that, and Thomas and his fellow servants were discharged with a mere undertaking to keep the peace for a further two years, on pain of a fine of five pounds. For those fellow accused who could not employ that defence, modest fines were administered that were payable within three months, failing which prison sentences would be imposed. They were all strictly admonished to behave themselves in future, since they could not expect to be so leniently dealt with a second time.

Then it was finally the turn of the leaders of the attempted breakaway, William Brewster, Richard Clyfton, John Robinson and William Bradford. The quarter sessions jury was composed of local men, many of whom sympathised with the plight of the Brownists, and some of whom shared their religious beliefs. The outcome was a finding of guilt accompanied by a plea for clemency, and the four men emerged from prison on a cold January morning in 1608, each with a ten-pound fine that was payable within three months. Default on payment would result in sixty days in prison.

There was a celebration as the four were cheered back into the old manor house that Thomas had partly restored. There was roast hog on the table, washed down with elderberry wine and accompanied by manchet bread flavoured with the nutmeg that Sarah had been saving for the occasion. The festivities were still underway when Thomas noticed William Brewster staring intently at him. The master indicated with a jerk of the head for Thomas to accompany him outside, and as they stood in the moonlight, Brewster placed a fatherly hand on Thomas's head.

'I wish you all the blessings that God can bestow upon you for your excellent service in preserving those most dear to me during our days of trial.'

'It was a pleasure, Master,' Thomas replied modestly, 'and in truth I was at the same time preserving myself. There is also the fact that I am bound to the service of not only your good self, but also your family.'

'How long does your indenture have to run, Thomas?' Brewster asked.

Thomas smiled. 'If truth be known, Master, it expired while you were being held in gaol.'

'But you did not exercise your freedom?'

'Why would I, when serving you is the only life I know? I hope that I am not about to be cast out?'

'Far from it, Thomas. I have in mind your elevation. Matthew Moore has advised me that he wishes to return to Scrooby along with his family. I have given him leave to do so, and I am therefore in need of a new steward. I would regard it as God's blessing were you to accept that position. In better times, it carried twenty pounds a year, but as matters lie…'

'I would gladly do it for nothing!' Thomas proclaimed.

'I believe that you would, Thomas, so here's my hand on it. On the morrow I will share with you a secret regarding our immediate future, but until then let us rejoin the company and make the joyful announcement.'

Late that night, the easterly gale that they had learned to dread hit them with renewed force, and the old barn that the household retainers were obliged to occupy rattled ominously. Thomas climbed into the former hayloft that he employed as a bedchamber of sorts, pulled the old horse blanket over his pitifully thin clothing and settled down to sleep as he contemplated his rise in material position and prayed hard that the barn would hold for at least one more night. He became aware of movement at his side, but before he could investigate whether it was the rats that also sought shelter in the barn, Amy slipped under the blanket with him.

'I'm frightened that I'm going freeze to death,' she complained, 'so can I share this blanket with you, even though it smells as if a horse is still inside it?'

Thomas slid slightly to one side, allowing Amy to share his warmth as she kissed him lightly on the cheek.

'So now you're steward to the Brewster household?' she asked.

'I am,' Thomas confirmed.

'So that makes you a free man?'

'It does.'

'A man who's free to marry?'

'Also true.'

'Have you given any thought to that?'

'On my first day of freedom? I have other matters that occupy my mind.'

'Such as who's going to be the new cook?'

'Do we need one?'

'Sarah Blount says she'll return to Scrooby with the Moore family. So, as the new steward, it'll be your job to find her replacement, won't it?'

Thomas chuckled. 'I think I begin to perceive your real reason for climbing into this hayloft. You wish me to recommend you for the vacant position of cook?'

'I also wish you to consider me for the vacant position of Mistress Bailey,' Amy added. 'You can claim the benefit of that this very night, if you like.'

Thomas sighed. 'I do not pretend to the devotion to God's word that Master Brewster espouses, but I know enough Scripture to have learned that fornication outside marriage is a sin.'

'But if you were to marry me soon after?'

Thomas held Amy more tightly as he kissed the top of her head. 'If it is within my power, you shall be the cook in due course. But I am not yet for marriage, so go to sleep and speak no more of it.'

5

Thomas was up before sunrise. He was in the process of sharpening his axe on the whetstone that had belonged to his carpenter father, and which he carried with him wherever he went, when he looked up at the sound of boots crunching through snow towards him.

'Up before the rest, as usual,' Brewster greeted him with a smile as he took a seat next to Thomas on the long bench that he'd constructed from old timber.

'It's a never-ending battle to keep the fires fed,' Thomas told him. 'Not just the ones that keep us warm, but those that Sarah requires if we are to eat.'

'I need to speak with you about the cook, now that you are my steward,' Brewster replied. 'Sarah has chosen to return with Matthew Moore to Scrooby, and I was wondering if Amy might be appointed in her place. Has she the skills?'

'So far as I can judge,' Thomas replied. 'Certainly she seems to know what she is about, and she is the only one available, is she not? If we are to remain here for any length of time, we will need her to fill our stomachs against the bitter weather.'

It fell silent for a moment. 'We may not be here for much longer, Thomas,' Brewster confided. 'I must insist that this remain a matter between we two only, but since you are now my steward you will need to play an important role in what is to follow.' He lowered his voice. 'I have by no means abandoned my ambition to see our entire congregation established in the Low Countries. That is also the wish of Pastor Clyfton, who as you know has been granted sanctuary in the house of Richard Smyth, leaving John Robinson to lead us in worship here. Through the good offices of Master Smyth, we are in communication with the same sea captain who successfully transported his brother across the Channel to Amsterdam, and there are plans afoot to make another attempt to slip from our bondage here.'

'But surely we're being closely watched?' Thomas objected. 'And we gave our bond for future good behaviour. Are you not also under threat of imprisonment if you do not pay that fine that was inflicted on you?'

'If all goes well, we shall all be well clear of here before that day arrives. As for the bonds you all gave, they will be matters for your own consciences, but Master Robinson advises that bonds given to Mammon may be broken if they conflict with one's duty towards God.'

'Even if that be so, how shall we escape detection?'

'It is proposed that we do not depart from Boston, and that we do not all slip away at the same time, and by the same road,' Brewster explained. 'The women and children will travel to Gainsborough, there to take to vessels that will conduct them down the Trent. Meanwhile, the men will travel north by road, as if on pilgrimage to York. We shall all then meet up again on the banks of the river they call the Humber, on the far bank from a town called Hull, there to take ship to Amsterdam.'

'And what role do you wish me to assume?' Thomas asked.

'A large party of women and children on the road would be a soft target for robbers and violators. They will need the protection of strong men, and I was advised of how you stood up against those blackguards who were threatening to ill-use some of our womenfolk when we were being brought back to Boston.'

'You wish me to accompany the party downriver from Gainsborough?' Thomas shook his head. 'I cannot undertake to do so alone.'

'I am aware of this, and will call for young men to accompany you, but under your command,' Brewster reassured him. 'Think of yourself as a warrior for God, if you will — a Templar Knight without the robes. But I do not need to emphasise the responsibility you will be undertaking, or the dangers to which you will be exposing yourself. It is as well that you have no wife and family depending upon you for their welfare. Were it otherwise, I would have grappled more thoroughly with my conscience before imposing upon you.'

'So you regard my unmarried state as a sign of my fitness to accept such an onerous burden?'

'In a sense, yes, I do. But it makes you no less a man, and your strength and courage are what we shall all be relying upon, if we are to reach Holland as a united congregation. You must, in turn, place your faith in God, and to assist in that I would ask that you join our inner congregation. It is time that we gave regard to how our "Church of God" is to be reorganised before we transfer to a new land, and I have long debated with John Robinson whether or not we should admit our womenfolk into the fold. He is in favour of that, as am I, with certain reservations, but if you are to undertake the solemn duty of guarding our weaker charges, then you must certainly be admitted to the congregation in order to receive your spiritual armour.'

The next few weeks confirmed what Thomas had already concluded for himself regarding the importance of obeying God's ordinance, living as pure a life as circumstances permitted, and standing up resolutely for what was right. He would never acquire the absolute zeal of the Puritan because his personality and upbringing tended to more practical matters, but he was content to let others take an inspired lead at the meetings while he committed himself to protecting them. He was proud to be among the congregation, which now included a select handful of women such as Mary Brewster and Bridget Robinson.

As the last of the winter snow faded into memory, plans for the second attempt to leave the country rapidly took form. It was left to each congregation member to advise their family of what was to happen in the near future, and in his capacity as steward Thomas was authorised to let the few remaining servants in on the secret. He called a short meeting in the crudely refurbished kitchen, and it fell quiet when he'd finished advising them of the plan for the women and children to form a separate group that would head for Gainsborough, then take boats on the River Trent that would convey them to the oceangoing vessel once they reached the Humber.

'Why are we travelling separately from the senior men?' Amy asked.

Thomas shrugged. 'Perhaps we'll be watched and followed when we leave, like we were last time. And it's the senior men who'll be the more tempting target for our persecutors. I think that the master's plan is devised to keep the rest of you safe, whatever may transpire.'

'And do we have to walk all the way to Gainsborough?' asked Mark Grantham, who had joined the household as a young boy to be trained as a coachman, but had since been helping Thomas around the grounds, while doing the heavy lifting for Amy in the kitchen.

Thomas shook his head. 'The wagons that we used when we stole out of Boston last year are being made available for our use again. The women, children and weaker members of our party will be able to sit in them until we get to Gainsborough.'

'And what will the master and the other congregation members be doing?' asked Alice Jones, the laundress.

'They'll be travelling directly to the Humber by road, to meet up with the ship and direct the captain upstream to where we'll join them,' said Thomas. 'But their women and children will be travelling with us, and we believe that our party will be close to sixty in number.'

'And you'll be leading us?' Amy asked hopefully, and when Thomas nodded, she smiled. 'Well, that's something, at least. We wouldn't want to place our lives at the mercy of young Master Jonathan.'

The next two weeks were spent packing and making ready the wagons. One morning during the first week Amy came into the kitchen, where Thomas was enjoying some hot bread from the oven, and advised him that there was a man outside who wished to speak with him. Thomas went to meet the visitor and introduced himself.

'I'm Henry Liggins,' the man told him, 'and I'm a boatman from Gainsborough. Your master's paid me to convey a group of you downriver into the Humber, where you'll meet with the rest of your party and take a ship to Holland. How many of you will there be?'

'Around sixty, all told,' Thomas replied, 'mainly women and children, but a few sturdy young boys.'

Liggins thought for a moment. 'If the boys are prepared to learn how to row, I can supply six boats, but it'll be a bit cramped, and a bit bumpy once we get into the Humber at Whitton.'

'We can endure that, I'm sure,' Thomas smiled. 'When do you want us to present ourselves at your moorings?'

'Make it two weeks today,' Liggins told him. 'I'm told you're meeting up with the rest of your party and taking a coastal barque downriver at Killingholme, so if we leave two weeks today we should be there on time. If you come down the riverbank once you cross the road that goes on towards Bawtry, you'll see my boats lined up ready for you.'

They shook hands, and Thomas called a meeting to advise everyone that they would be taking to the wagons again in two weeks' time and heading into Gainsborough in order to sail out to the Humber. He then called Amy to join him in making plans for the food they'd need to take.

She came over and planted a kiss on his cheek. 'Quite the brave leader these days,' she purred. 'If it gets cold while we're sailing down the Trent, can I snuggle up to you again?'

'Only if you genuinely need to do so in order to keep warm,' Thomas replied gently. There had been no repeat of that occasion during the previous winter when she'd spent the night under his horse blanket, and if anything she'd been a little cool towards him in the intervening months. He'd heard idle gossip passing between other household staff that she might have taken a fancy to Mark Grantham, the youth who helped out in the kitchen among his other jobs, but it had not occurred to Thomas to make further enquiry.

The day of departure arrived: a frosty morning in April of 1608. There were tearful farewells, pleas from fathers who were entrusting their wives and offspring to Thomas's care that he watch over them carefully, and last-minute loading of the essentials that they had required until the final moment. Amy had proved her value to the community by organising most of the women into a flurry of baking, while she wrapped the remaining meat supplies for their sustenance during the week-long journey. After a final wave and a few wails of apprehension, Thomas led the slow procession northwards from the back of a borrowed horse.

They reached the rendezvous point in Gainsborough more quickly than they had anticipated. Henry Liggins led them to the boats lined up by the bank, leaving Thomas to decide who was to travel in which vessel.

An hour later, they cast off with the assistance of a south-westerly wind that allowed the modest sails to waft them downstream. The Trent was tidal at this point, and the outgoing tide was in their favour as they glided past fields, small woods and raised hillocks, each of which seemed to be the site of a modest village. Even when the tide began to change, the wind didn't, and with a little additional assistance from oars pulled by eager novices, they managed to make further progress until night fell. They then climbed onto the riverbank to huddle together under the covers they had brought along, after a modest meal that was passed around by eager hands. Each woman in the party accepted responsibility for collecting what they required and ensuring that their children ate.

It went on like this for several days, and by the time they glided out into the upper estuary of the Humber, they were still at least a day ahead of that set for their reunion with the men who had travelled directly by road, and would be trailing them a few miles to the east as they took the overland route. Then things began to go awry.

Although the open sea was still some distance to the east of them, several miles downstream on the Humber, the estuary was a wider stretch of water than many of them had ever experienced. The wind had turned easterly on the changing tide, rocking their flimsy river boats between incoming waves. Many of the women and children were vomiting over the gunnels within thirty minutes of reaching the open water, and as they grew weaker, they took to lying in the scuppers, dry-retching and groaning.

Amy looked pleadingly at Thomas. 'We can't be expected to survive much more of this,' she complained as she made another lurch for the gunnels.

Thomas turned to Liggins, who was commanding the rudder at the stern. 'We clearly can't sit it out here for another day,' he told him, 'so can we put ashore somewhere and wait?'

Liggins nodded downstream to his right. 'There's some sort of creek down yonder, where all the trees are, so we'll pull into there and go ashore until the rest of your party shows up.'

The travellers needed no persuasion as the vessels steered towards the southern bank of the estuary and into a narrow creek that was overhung with trees, many of them willows. They stepped gratefully onto the sand, and Liggins ordered all the boats to be beached a good ten feet above where the waves were lapping onto the shore, in order to prevent them being pulled back out into the stream and stolen by the outgoing tide a few hours later.

The following morning the party discovered that their boats were stuck in mud that had hardened to the consistency of rock. They could not be budged in order to continue the journey downstream to meet up with the large ocean-going vessel whose sails became visible towards the middle of the day, at least a mile down the lengthy rock-strewn beach. Reaching the larger vessel's party on foot was likely to be hard, with long stretches of deep, treacherous sand in between.

Thomas ordered Mark to remain with his billhook to protect the rest of the party against any wild animals that might be lurking in the trees in which they had set up a camp. He then set off at the best pace of which he was capable. Within minutes, his calves were aching from the effort of pushing his feet through deep, muddy sand, and he was contemplating a return to the camp when he heard a shout in the distance. He looked up, and there was John Robinson, standing on a rock and waving. Thomas waved back and shouted, and the two men began stumbling towards each other.

'We thought you were all lost,' Robinson declared breathlessly as he grasped Thomas's hand in greeting.

'The women were feeling ill from the motion of the boats,' Thomas told him, 'so we landed in a creek further upstream there. Now I know that we may all come together again as one party, I'll go and get them. We may have to walk, because the boats are wedged into the bank and we couldn't move them.'

'I'll alert the master to the situation,' Robinson replied.

Thomas stumbled back to his party, then when his legs gave out Amy ordered him to rest them for a short while. She insisted that she was more than capable of organising their party to prepare to walk down to where they would board the ship.

When Thomas was fully rested, he rose to his feet and took a few moments to reassure his nervous companions. 'The ship awaits us down there, along with the men who have made it safely from Gainsborough. We now need to walk along the shoreline to meet them, and then we may board the ship and leave this unfriendly land.'

'Not just yet, you won't!' a voice rang out. A large body of men emerged from the trees, armed with long pikes, muskets and swords.

'I'm Senior Constable Davey of the County Watch,' their leader announced, 'and these are my men. You all stay where you are, because you're being taken in charge!'

6

It was chaos, with children screaming, mothers clutching them, and the few young men who were in the party looking to Thomas for guidance. He raised his hand, and it slowly fell silent as he looked defiantly into the eyes of Senior Constable Davey.

'What are your orders?' he demanded.

Davey nodded towards the sails in the distance. 'Other than to prevent you boarding that vessel, none.'

'So if we depart peacefully from this place, none of your men will seek to harm any of these good folk?'

'That is the case, but we must first be seen to escort you back to Grimsby, where we are based, in order to discharge the duty we were given.'

'Who betrayed us?' Thomas demanded.

Davey shook his head. 'I know not, but even if I did, I would not be allowed to disclose their name. I know only that you were seeking to escape the realm on that ship out there, and for that I must escort you back to answer questions regarding those who plotted to make that possible.'

'I am the only one who knows, and I will tell you nothing,' Thomas insisted.

Davey smiled. 'As a man of the true faith, I am heartened to hear you say that. Now, once we have been joined by the men I see running up the foreshore towards us, we must be off.'

While Davey had been securing the detention of the main party of women and children, Brewster, Robinson and the male group had been watching from a distance, horror-stricken. Then, as they stood debating what they might do, a ship's boat had been lowered from the Dutch vessel that had arrived to transport them to Amsterdam, and its captain had called out to them from the shallows.

'The tide will soon be against us. We must now leave! Come first with your best men, and I will return!'

Brewster looked helplessly from side to side. On the one hand, here was the vessel that would finally free them from religious persecution and afford them a new life in the Low Countries. But a mile upstream were his wife and two young daughters, Patience and Fear, and his heart heaved at the thought of abandoning them to possible imprisonment and torture. It was John Robinson who finally convinced him.

'William, we cannot abandon our families now!'

Brewster turned to the remainder of his party. 'Jonathan, Richard Clyfton, William Bradford, Samuel Fuller and Moses Fletcher, board that vessel and establish a base for us in Amsterdam. John Robinson, Edward Winslow, Isaac Allerton and all the rest of you, follow me back to your families up there, to share their fate. Jonathan, embrace your father, perhaps for the last time, and acquit yourself well in the Lord's work in the new land. We will join you when the Lord allows, and William Bradford is to replace John Robinson as assistant pastor until we are once again reunited. Go now, quickly!'

Those ordered to leave waded through the shallows and climbed into the ship's boat, which was hastily rowed out into midstream, where the square-rigged barque awaited them, the deckhands in the process of hauling canvas aloft. The anchor was raised, and as the vessel began to move towards the open ocean, Brewster turned to those who had remained.

'Come, gentlemen, and let us see what other tribulations the Lord has prepared for us.'

They staggered through the sand towards the captured group and were offered no resistance as they clasped their loved ones to them. Brewster picked out Davey as the head of their captors and asked, 'Where are you taking us?'

'Grimsby, to the south of here,' he was told, 'but we have wagons in the lane out there.'

The sun had given way to a watery half-moon by the time the magistrate in the fishing port had testily advised Davey that there were not enough cells in his courthouse to accommodate the fifty or so assorted men, women and children that he had brought in. To Brewster's surprise, Davey smiled, as if this was the outcome he had been expecting, and led everyone back outside onto the cobbles.

'You will all remain here until daylight,' he instructed them, 'but if you are not here when the sun rises, rest assured we shall not come looking for you, since we have better things to do.'

Brewster and Thomas were still debating whether it was worth trying to escape when they became aware of a small group of men sidling onto the road in front of their larger group. One of them called out to five others, who sidled up to join him, followed by even more. There were eventually almost twenty men looking enquiringly at them, then one of them spoke.

'Is your leader one William Brewster?'

'I am he,' Brewster announced as he stepped forward.

'You are the man who sought to lead a congregation of Separatists out of the realm?'

'No, that was me,' Thomas insisted as he stepped in front of Brewster. 'If you are seeking someone at whom to hurl insults, or perhaps rocks, then I am your man. But be warned that I have been known to fell a man with one blow!'

'Softly, Thomas,' Brewster urged from behind him. 'That is not the Christian way you have been taught, remember?'

The man who had demanded the identity of their leader smiled. 'You, I take it, are the true leader of your congregation, whatever idle boasts this loudmouth may make?'

'I am its convener, certainly,' Brewster admitted, 'but the preaching of the true word is vouchsafed to others.'

'You can read and write, I am informed,' the man persisted.

Brewster nodded. 'I am so blessed, since by such means I may study the psalms and other righteous works.'

'I have a use for your services, should you be minded to turn your hand to the copying of worthy tomes,' the man told him. 'My name is Fortitude Jenkins.'

Brewster's face lit up as he recognised the name of the man who, almost single-handedly, had laboured for many years to make copies of religious tracts available to congregations such as the one that had met secretly in Scrooby. 'If you be who I believe you to be, then I would happily undertake to work with you, but I have a wife and two daughters here with me.'

'They may be accommodated with you in my workshop, should they be not too proud to be housed in such a fashion,' Jenkins replied.

'Pride is a sin before God, and in truth to even have a sound roof over their heads would be a vast improvement on what they have known these past weeks.'

'Then it is decided.' Jenkins extended an arm to his right. 'If you would care to accompany me, I will direct you all to your new abode, and see that you are fed.'

'But I cannot abandon those who accompany me to whatever fate may befall them, left out here in the street in a strange town,' Brewster objected.

'These men who accompany *me* have made a commitment to God similar to mine. They learned, through the good offices of the local constable, that you were to be brought here among us,' Jenkins assured him. 'Each of them wishes to offer work to those of your assembly who are suitably qualified, and in many instances, they may be able to house them.'

'I'll take the loudmouth!' called a heavy-set man with a beard down to the middle of his chest. 'You need to be tough in my line of business. Do you know anything about fish, you with the big fists?'

'I used to catch perch in the local river,' Thomas replied.

The big man laughed. 'If you come to work for me, you'll be heaving boxes of cod and haddock around the harbourside, and making sure that nobody pinches them. My name is Daniel Petersen.'

'And you have somewhere I can live and eat?' Thomas asked.

'Yes,' Petersen replied, 'although you'll soon get tired of eating fish.'

'Do you also need a cook?' Amy asked as she stepped forward, but Petersen shook his head.

'I do!' shouted another man. Following a brief exchange, Amy had been hired to provide meals for a family of seven born to a local merchant whose wife had died the previous year. One by one, those standing outside the courthouse had found employment, and dispersed with their new employers into the moonlit streets of Grimsby.

'This was no chance encounter, was it?' Brewster asked of Jenkins as he and his family walked alongside him to the workshop on Freeman Lane.

'Indeed it was not,' Jenkins confirmed. 'We learned of your intention to take ship to Amsterdam when my brother-in-law Richard Davey was given the order to apprehend you.'

'The senior constable who showed us such forbearance in the matter of our arrest?'

'The very same. A man committed to God, in his own way, but not one of our congregation.'

'God be praised!' whispered Brewster. 'You are a Separatist yourself?'

'These many years, which is why I have devoted many of my working days to the dissemination of religious works, while undertaking commissions for the university at Cambridge. You are familiar with the moveable type printing press?'

'No, I fear not.'

'This will not be a problem, since I do all the pressing. What I will require from you is the patience and skill to assemble lines of letters onto a page. It is a process similar to writing, except that the letters are already formed, on blocks of wood. It is very tiring for the eyes, and mine have suffered in consequence, which is why I now have need of yours. But above where you will be working and sleeping is a large room where we assemble for our worship, to which your own congregation will be welcome. Our numbers have fallen somewhat since the recent persecutions.'

'How will I reach out to those of my former congregation who are now spread widely around your town?' Brewster asked.

'Those who gave them employment and a roof over their heads are members of our humble gathering, and they will bring them in.'

'God does indeed move in mysterious ways,' Brewster murmured, as he turned to his wife and elder daughter. 'Mary, Patience, be sure, during your bedtime prayers, to thank Almighty God for His blessed mercy in bringing His children out of bondage.' He turned back to Jenkins. 'But what of the constables?' he asked.

'They will not seek you further, as Richard Davey hinted when he led you outside to meet us. They have fulfilled their obligations by preventing you from sailing. Nor will they trouble themselves to investigate your gradual departure from our midst.' Jenkins lowered his voice. 'You did not think that your remaining days were to be spent in this fishing port, did you? Where there is a port, there are vessels. Vessels, what is more, that regularly put to sea for days at a time and head for the fishing grounds south of here.'

'You would assist us, even yet, to reach Amsterdam?'

'Of course, which is why Daniel Petersen sought out the man who seemed to be the bravest among you — or the most foolhardy. Either way, he will be employed in your final escape, although it must be in small groups, the ordering of which I shall leave to your good self.'

Several days later, amid joyful expressions of praise and gratitude to God, the members of the former Scrooby congregation were reunited. They were part of a wider group that met above the printing room in which Brewster was now working.

Thomas had only been employed in stacking and guarding boxes of fish belonging to his employer for two weeks when he was invited on board one of the vessels by Petersen. She was called the *Lady Elizabeth*, and with three sets of mainsails and a spinnaker, she looked more like an armed merchantman than a coastal fishing trawler. Petersen took him below decks into the fish hold, where the smell was overpowering even though it was currently empty.

Petersen waved his arm towards the far bulwarks and asked, 'How many folk do you reckon you could fit in here, at a push?'

'Why?' Thomas asked.

Petersen frowned. 'I ask the questions round here. Now, how many, do you reckon?'

Thomas looked round carefully before replying, 'No more than eight or ten, why?'

'One more question, lad — ever been to sea?'

'No — and again, why?'

'For a man that's only fit for heaving fish crates around, you ask a lot of questions. Has that leader of yours not told you yet?'

'Told me what?'

'Go and ask him. But do it today, because we set sail on the morning tide.'

Thomas went back on deck, then jumped across onto the quayside and walked towards the stack of boxes he'd been guarding until invited onto the *Lady Elizabeth*. A carter's wagon was trundling towards him, its driver carrying a consignment note from a local fish merchant, and suddenly the boy sitting next to him called out Thomas's name and jumped down from the wagon before it had even come to a rest.

Thomas shook hands with Mark Grantham, then nodded towards the wagon. 'So you're now a carter's boy?'

'That's right,' Mark grinned. 'It's a good living, and my new master's kind to me in his own way, so I can't complain. What about you — are these your fish?'

'My master's,' Thomas told him. 'But tell me, what became of the others from Master Brewster's household?'

'Didn't Amy keep you informed?'

'I haven't seen her since she went to work as a cook for that man who chose her outside the courthouse,' said Thomas.

Mark blushed. 'Forgive me — I was led to believe that she was your woman.'

'Not by her, surely?'

'No, by the cook that went back to Scrooby. Amy was making up to me, or so I thought, and Sarah warned me that she was only doing that in order to make you pay more attention to her. I just assumed that you had come together when she began to speak coolly to me again.'

Thomas chuckled. 'I'm not interested in her, as she must surely have learned by now, so you may feel at liberty to pursue her affections.'

Mark looked sheepishly at the ground. 'I've got other fish to fry. My new master's got a beautiful daughter. Catherine, her name is, and from the looks she gives me, I think I might have a chance of capturing her interest.'

'Good luck with that,' Thomas laughed. 'Now, how about lifting some of these boxes, before the father of the beautiful Catherine decides to whip you into action?'

After seeing the consignment safely loaded and driven away, Thomas walked off the quayside and into Freeman Lane. He had been in regular attendance at the twice-weekly meetings of the Scrooby Separatists, but Brewster had said nothing about any need to hide people in fish holds. He found his erstwhile master huddled over a line of wooden blocks in the printing room, and had to raise his voice to be heard above the clattering of the metal press in the corner that was being opened and closed by Fortitude Jenkins.

'Master, why does Daniel Petersen wish to know how many can be squeezed into an evil-smelling fish hold?' Thomas asked.

Brewster sighed and turned away from his work. 'He was meant to leave it to me to explain, but I have a most solemn task to impose on you, should you be willing. It will involve some risk, and not a little travel.'

'The travel will begin tomorrow, or so it would seem,' Thomas replied with a frown. 'I am to put to sea with Petersen, yet I know nothing of how to employ fishing nets, nor how to raise and lower ships' sails.'

'You will not be required to,' Brewster replied. 'You will have the duty of ensuring the safe loading and unloading of passengers — loading them here, then unloading them in Amsterdam.'

'You still think we should journey to the Low Countries?'

'More than ever, now that God has shown us the way. I will select each group and send them to you on the quayside shortly before you are due to set sail. You will hide them in the hold until you are safely out to sea, then you will escort them back on deck and ensure that they come to no harm. Once in Amsterdam there will be someone to guide them through the city to the safety of those who have undertaken to supply them with shelter, and perhaps some employment. They will carry letters of introduction from me.'

'Who is the man in Amsterdam?'

'I know not, but he will make himself known to you. He has been told to look out for the vessel when it docks, and Captain Petersen has already delivered a letter from me to William

Bradford, who made known his current address in Amsterdam to his cousin in Scrooby. He in turn passed it to Richard Smyth in Gainsborough, who knew of the events that overtook us in the Humber and was able to pass the letter to our good friend in God Fortitude Jenkins over there. I take the safe arrival of that letter as a further sign from God that He is with us at this time.'

'When will the first party be ready to leave?'

'When I learn from Petersen that you have acquired your sea legs. God speed your voyage tomorrow, and remember each night to commit your safety to He who walked upon the waters of Galilee.'

The following day, once the *Lady Elizabeth* was a league out to sea, riding in the face of a strong northerly gale, Thomas grimly concluded that walking on water would be a simple achievement compared with attempting to remain upright on a bucking deck. He clung grimly to the gunnels while the half a dozen deckhands grinned at his discomfort.

'At least you're not throwing up yet,' one of them reminded him sympathetically, just as Thomas leaned over the side to release his breakfast. It seemed to go on like this for hours until the swell suddenly changed from a deep rolling motion into something choppier and shallower.

Petersen strode confidently towards him, his experienced sea legs automatically compensating for the movement of the deck. 'How do you like life at sea, then?'

'I'll stick to the land,' Thomas told him as he swallowed more bile.

Petersen nodded over the port bow. 'See that grey line out there? That's the Low Countries, but we'll be turning back this time. Just wanted you to get an idea of what each of the short voyages will be like.'

Thomas groaned. There would, by his calculation, be at least five of these terrible journeys before everyone was safely transferred to Amsterdam, and almost instinctively he offered up a prayer to God to give him the strength to play his humble part in the fulfilment of Brewster's ambition. Perhaps, once he was settled in the new land, he could decide for himself what trade he might follow. One day he might even become a husband and father, always assuming that he was not destined for a watery grave.

The first group of eight came on board the *Lady Elizabeth* two weeks later, by which time Thomas was capable of making the journey out into the southern reaches of the North Sea without vomiting or falling over. He already detested the smell of fish, but he was grateful that he'd been afforded the opportunity to acclimatise to life at sea before he oversaw the welfare of the incoming passengers.

Given the state of the wind and tide, it was necessary to time the first embarkation during the hours of darkness, and the two families that had been selected for the first journey had to be all but forced down into the evil-smelling hold. They eventually came back up on deck three leagues out to sea, throwing up as they tried desperately to maintain their footing.

The father of the family looked accusingly at Thomas. 'We have learned to trust you, Master Bailey, but you test our faith in you with this wretched hazard.'

They were less resentful when the sun rose to their left as they glided into a mooring on the jetty at Amsterdam. The familiar figure of William Bradford could be seen standing beside a stack of timber on the quayside. Thomas leapt gleefully off the deck of the *Lady Elizabeth* and grasped William's hand in a warm greeting.

'You took the easy part, as usual,' he jested, but William shook his head. 'You will not say that once you have been a month in this unfamiliar place. I have found work and shelter for those bedraggled wretches that I see glowering at me from your deck, but I doubt they will thank either of us for what we have brought them to.'

'All is not as promised?' Thomas asked.

William shrugged. 'It is what you make of it, as with all things in this life. At least you have not drowned; God must have a reason for allowing you to land.'

'I shall not be tarrying on this occasion,' Thomas told him, 'since it is Master Brewster's instruction that I give the Good Lord further opportunities to drown me. We shall send word of when you will receive the next group, and in the meantime, I should be grateful if you would point me in the direction of some hostelry where God will not have a chance to poison me.'

Five months elapsed before the final human cargo was smuggled below decks on the *Lady Elizabeth*, and it consisted of the Brewster family and the remains of their former household. Thomas gave a silent prayer of thanks that this would be his final miserable ordeal at sea as he held out his hand to help Amy Tasker over the side. As she leaned in, she gave him a peck on the cheek. 'So this is what became of you, is it? Fishing? Did you find yourself a woman yet, or did the smell of haddock put them all off you?'

'You will experience the smell of haddock soon enough,' Thomas teased as he nodded towards the hatch above the hold. 'Just pray that this fine weather holds, since I recall your throwing up in even the mild waters of the Humber.'

William Brewster, the last to climb aboard, grasped Thomas's hand in gratitude. 'You have performed excellently in the Lord's service, Thomas,' he praised him, 'and we may this day begin the next stage of our lives knowing that you are ever there to provide us with material protection.'

As the vessel cast off, and the last of the deckhands descended from the rigging after securing full sail, Thomas allowed himself one final look back at the land of his birth. He seemed to have lived the first twenty years of his life in the service of others, and he wondered if one day he might be allowed to determine his own destiny.

7

When the Brewster household arrived in Amsterdam, Thomas climbed unsteadily onto the quayside to gaze in awe at the fine buildings behind the Oosterdok, as the main harbour was called. John Robinson was waiting to greet the party, along with a few strangers who spoke little English.

Amsterdam was far from being a simple fishing port, and it possessed a vast number of wharves, staithes, yards and storage sheds, while goods were passing to and fro constantly, requiring men of stamina to unload wagons, roll barrels, and manhandle crates and boxes. Thomas was therefore employed by the end of his first day off the boat.

He took lodgings in a long five-bedded dormitory above the offices of his dockside employer, and as the sun was casting its last rays on the roofs of the houses in the Prins Hendrikkade behind the harbour, Thomas was sitting by the front door, peeling an apple. He suddenly heard his name being called and saw William Bradford hurrying towards him.

'William!' he replied gleefully as he scrambled to his feet to shake his friend's hand. 'How fare things with you?'

'Middling well,' the young man replied. 'I am here to invite you to our meeting this evening. It is also our *first* meeting since our arrival here.'

'The congregation is being reunited in worship?'

'Indeed it is — the first action of William Brewster when he came from the boat was to enquire after premises in which he and his family might abide, and which were large enough to host a meeting of the faithful.'

'Was there not a congregation here already?' Thomas asked.

Bradford shrugged. 'Indeed there *was*, after a fashion. But Pastor Robinson counselled Master Brewster against joining it. He urged him instead to establish his own meeting room in which those of us who came from Scrooby might keep the faith. There are many abandoned buildings here in Amsterdam that were once secret churches in the days when Catholics worshipped under the noses of the authorities. They were tolerated because the Spanish ruled here until only recently, and the authorities thought it better not to challenge their existence provided they were discreet. They are called "schuilkerken", and Master Brewster was able to secure one for a bargain rental only a few streets away from here, to where I am to convey you.'

The two men walked steadily through the dusk to what looked like a merchant warehouse in Valkenburgerstraat. They knocked on the front door, which was opened for them by Jonathan Brewster. He frowned when he saw who was being admitted. 'Father will be *so* pleased to see you both in such excellent company,' he said sarcastically.

William Brewster came out of the rear room with a broad smile and an extended hand. 'So good to see you again, Thomas! William found you, then?'

'Clearly he did,' Thomas smiled back, 'and to judge by the sound of voices through yonder door, he found a few others as well.'

'We are fortunate that Amsterdam is such a close-knit community that respects virtue, thrift and honest toil,' said Brewster. 'We were able to find employment for almost everyone, including your former fellow estate worker Amy, who is now providing excellent meals for one of the wealthiest families in town. As for the rest, they have been set to learn new trades, my own son included; he is busy acquiring the secrets of ribbon-making. I myself have been fortunate to have had an introduction to a local printing house, although since I do not speak Dutch, I can only be employed in selected works for which my knowledge of English is highly valued.'

'And William here tells me that this is the first meeting of the full congregation,' Thomas said as he nodded towards the open door.

Brewster shook his head sadly. 'Less than twenty at present, so hardly the full congregation. I have asked Pastor Robinson to lead us in prayer, since Richard Clyfton took to attending the congregation that John Smyth established here last year with his Gainsborough followers, although I gather that there is a widening gulf in their respective beliefs. But come inside and let us begin our worship.'

In the rear room, Thomas was met with muted cheers as he appeared back among those whose passage across to the Low Countries he had organised and protected. He nodded and smiled back at almost all of them, mainly men. He remained at the back while William Bradford stepped eagerly to the front row and nodded to John Robinson that it was time to begin.

An hour later, Thomas had renewed his link with God after a lapse of some months and was cheered by the warm glow that once again seemed to envelop him as he heard the familiar words of the favoured Psalms. He listened to John Robinson compare the small band of which Thomas was an accepted member with the disciples who had followed Christ. Robinson also claimed that the Separatist movement generally was no different from the tribe led by Moses from the bondage of Ancient Egypt into the Promised Land.

Later, as they broke bread around the long table in the upper room, Thomas was reminded of the Last Supper, and he called down the table to Brewster. 'Are we really to be likened to the Children of Israel, Master?'

'We are indeed,' Brewster assured him. 'Are we not in an unfamiliar land to which we have brought our own simple, honest form of worship? But please do not continue to call me "Master", since you have obviously not been in my direct service since our days in Grimsby. However, there is not a man or woman around this table who would not willingly admit that you were of great service to us all, in giving us safe passage across the Channel.'

'It was my own humble way of assisting in God's work,' Thomas replied, 'and being back here among so many honest and upright friends has made me realise that there is a blessing in community, and strength to be gained from receiving God's word in congregation.'

'Would that all our fellow travellers on the road to God's truth felt the same,' John Robinson intervened sadly.

Brewster sighed. 'John, as ever, speaks truth,' he murmured. 'You should know, Thomas, since you have done so much to ensure that our congregation remains together, that there are deep divisions emerging within it that can only be regarded as the Devil's own work in causing chaos and upheaval.'

'Whence come these divisions of which you speak?' Thomas asked. 'This evening's worship seemed as united as ever.'

'As indeed it is, inside these walls,' Brewster conceded. 'But, much as it pains me to have to relate, our own Pastor Clyfton has taken issue with John Smyth regarding the matter of infant baptism.'

'I was aware that he is against it,' Thomas replied, 'and that John Smyth favours it, but how can that have widened into such a gulf that it threatens to split our community? Was it not in the hope of combining our congregation with that of Smyth's Gainsborough flock that we first left Scrooby?'

'Indeed it was,' John Robinson confirmed, 'and please God we shall all one day remember that, before the true religion is split asunder in the same way that Moses parted the waters of the Red Sea.'

'Might I enquire if this dissension is the reason why Pastor Robinson led our worship this evening, and not Pastor Clyfton, as was once our practice?' Thomas ventured.

'You may indeed,' said Brewster, 'and you would be correct. It is a matter of considerable regret to me that I was prevailed upon, as one of my first tasks for my current employer, to set up a manuscript by Pastor Clyfton in which he argued that baptism should be reserved for true converts to God's ways only in their adult years, when they have heard the call. In that I concur, but it runs contrary to the views of John Smyth, and he forbade Clyfton to attend any more of his meetings.'

'Then why is Pastor Clyfton not back here amongst us?' Thomas asked.

Robinson coughed uneasily. 'Regrettably, Pastor Clyfton has become anathema to those who now call themselves "Baptists", among whom may be listed John Smyth himself. When he was cast out of Smyth's congregation, Pastor Clyfton joined a sect here who call themselves "Mennonites", although some of their number also prefer to call themselves "Anabaptists". It was Master Brewster here who persuaded me that we should not be seen to take up with either group, but should contain ourselves within our own congregation, whose religious views are internally harmonious.'

'So we are now our own church?' Thomas asked.

Robinson nodded. 'Are you minded to remain with us, or do you also entertain doubts such as those that have afflicted Pastor Clyfton in his old age?'

'You credit me with too much depth of thought,' Thomas said, blushing. 'I know only that when I stand for worship with those I have known for many years, I feel an inner warmth and comfort that comes, I believe, from the love of God passing silently through our gatherings.'

'So beautifully put,' Robinson murmured. 'While you are so inspired, have you a name you might suggest for this new form of worship?'

'We are our own congregation, are we not?' said Thomas after a moment's thought. 'A group of believers who are united for the purpose of worshipping God with one voice? And we would grant the same blessing to any other congregation that feels so inspired?'

'Indeed,' Robinson replied encouragingly.

'Then surely we should call ourselves "Congregationalists", should we not?'

Brewster smiled warmly. 'Not only have you proved yourself to be our material guardian these past few years, but now you have defined our religion. Yours must surely be the voice of God calling down to us, Thomas.'

Thomas was still feeling embarrassed and unworthy of such high praise as he walked back towards his lodgings above the shipping office. William Bradford walked excitedly alongside him, obviously anxious to talk.

'I once chided you for your lack of letters, Thomas, but this night I have learned that one may serve the Lord in many ways, and that yours may well be the purist heart amongst us, given that God spoke through you in that way. I thank Him for putting into your mouth the belief that I have long espoused in my heart. We are a small congregation, but nonetheless a pure one, and you have aptly named us.'

'In truth, I was merely giving voice to what was in my mind,' Thomas admitted. 'I am sad to see the lines of discord driven through what should be a congregation that speaks with one voice. What is happening to the united group that left Scrooby with such high ambitions puts me in mind of the humble dandelion. It grows on a single stalk, as once did our so-called "Separatist" movement. Then when it reaches full maturity, its head contains many separate but delicate flowers, as with our congregation when it sought to join with that in Gainsborough. Then along comes a strong wind, and all its thousands of carefully crafted seeds are blown in all directions, leaving the stalk that nurtured them to wither and die.'

'A poet as well as a man of action,' Bradford murmured appreciatively. 'You should consider standing up at our meetings when the inspiration urges you — it is truly how our worship is meant to be conducted.'

'Now I fear you are in danger of mocking me,' Thomas replied dismissively. 'But here is my lodging, and I am minded to kneel to God before my humble pallet and thank Him for allowing me to be his instrument. I may then return to serving Him with the brawn of my arm rather than the wanderings of my mind.'

Three days later, Thomas was sent with a wagon to the House of de Kuyper, a wealthy silk establishment along the Herengracht Canal, one of many that ringed the old town and linked it with the harbour. He was unloading the bales of raw silk that had just been offloaded from a deep ocean barque belonging to his employer, when he heard the shrill laughter of a young woman. He looked up and smiled with genuine affection as Amy Tasker skipped up the side alley, dodged the silk bales and flung her arms around him, planting a kiss on his lips.

'So *that's* where you got to, Thomas Bailey! But you couldn't continue with your new life without visiting me one last time, could you? You're even thinner than I remember, which is more than I can say for myself.'

'You live here?' Thomas asked as he gazed up at the merchant's four-storey house.

Amy nodded enthusiastically. 'On the top floor, with the other servants. I cook for the de Kuyper family, which I'll be joining soon, unless you're minded to make me a better offer.'

Thomas looked puzzled, so Amy explained further.

'Remember I said that this would be your last visit to me? Indeed it will, for I will no longer be Amy Tasker the Cook. The master's youngest son has asked for my hand in marriage, so when you next call — assuming that it'd be proper for a lady of the house to consort with a mere wagon driver — I'll be the good wife of Arnoud de Kuyper. Unless, of course, you still wish to claim me for yourself, although I might need more persuading than I might've done when we were both in service together in Scrooby.'

'This is wonderful news, Amy!' Thomas replied, genuinely pleased for her and experiencing no jealousy whatever. 'I take it that you love this man?'

'Maybe I'll get round to that in due course,' Amy replied with a mischievous twinkle in her eye. 'Not in the same way I once loved you, Thomas Bailey, and perhaps still do, if put to the question.'

'How can you give yourself to a man you do not love?' Thomas asked, appalled.

Amy's smile faded. 'You still believe all that flummery about God in his Heaven? That one shouldn't do the business without a meeting of souls? Well, hear this, *Saint* Thomas — I'll be twenty-one on my next birthday, and if I am to know the joy of children, then it's time I took a husband. The position was offered to you more than once, had your thoughts ever strayed beyond your precious church, and had your mind been open to the signals that my body was sending you. Don't blush like that — it's important that you learn to understand women, Thomas. One day there'll be another like me, who sends you the same signals, but if your head's still in the clouds then you'll miss them. You're too fine in the body not to leave children behind you, so bring your thoughts down to earth, give me a farewell kiss, and wish me years of happiness as the wife of a wealthy man and the mother of lots of children.'

Thomas embraced her, wished her God's blessings, despite her earlier dismissal of religion, and savoured the kiss that landed fleetingly on his lips before Amy hurried back down the alleyway.

He watched her go without any pangs of regret, but wondered whether he was receiving another message from on high.

8

Life continued as normal for the recently re-established congregation that met in Brewster's schuilkerken until the financial struggle almost overwhelmed them. They had all been contributing communally to the upkeep of the old building, but there was also the matter of the living expenses of William Brewster himself, his wife and three offspring.

Jonathan was able to hand over a few guilders a week, but he did so grudgingly, since he was still apprenticed to the ribbon maker down the road. He received little in the way of reward other than a modest midday meal that was far beneath the standard to which he been accustomed back in Scrooby, and he never failed to express his resentment at the family's straitened circumstances. His father's fortunes varied according to the commissions in the English language awarded to his printer employer, but there never seemed to be enough to support any form of tolerable lifestyle for his wife Mary and their other two children.

As for the other members of the congregation, most of whom had families of their own, it was a struggle to put food into their own mouths from the pittances they were earning in various trades. Most of them were associated with the textile industries for which the Low Countries had always been renowned. Only William Bradford seemed to be earning a solid income from his rapidly acquired skill in fustian manufacture, and his breeches were being worn on the calves and thighs of some of the more prominent merchants around the thriving town.

Even John Robinson felt obliged to make a financial contribution towards the congregation of which he was the pastor, and before long his learning earned him a position at nearby Leiden University, holding classes for students of English and Theology. He also obtained occasional teaching work for William Brewster, but given that the journey between Amsterdam and Leiden could take up to a day, depending on the condition of the roads, it was not an attractive alternative for a family man with worrying memories of persecution for his faith.

Over the following year, the Brewster family relied more and more on Thomas. He contributed what amounted to two-thirds of his earnings towards the upkeep of the congregation and lent his muscle whenever the church required donated furniture to be collected by wagon. He also carried out repairs to the roof, and guarded the church's doors against prying eyes on meeting nights.

One evening after work, Thomas was lying on his pallet in the room above the shipping office, staring at the uneven wall, when Jacobus, the man who ran the business on the ground floor and gave the men their daily orders, clumped up the stairs and called out to him.

'There is a woman seeking you!'

Thomas wandered down the stairs and out onto the cobbles in front of the shipping office, where he was confronted by a much altered Amy Tasker.

She was dishevelled and had an old blanket draped around her shoulders. Her once flaxen hair was smeared with drying blood, and there was a cut along one eyebrow, while the cheekbone below it was heavily bruised. One side of her face was swollen to twice its size, and Thomas barely recognised her for a moment. When he did, he hurried towards her with a shout of disbelief; her reaction was to throw herself into his arms and gabble hysterically.

Thomas stood back and placed his hands on her shoulders. 'More slowly. What has happened? Have you been set upon? Why did you not run home to the protection of your husband?'

'It was him who left me like this!' she wailed. 'Two hours since. I've been walking the streets since then.'

Thomas was dumbstruck. 'Your own husband did this to you?'

Amy's face crumpled in misery. 'He always does this, when … when … it's his way of enjoying my body.'

'You are telling me that when you and he … that is, when you … you and he are engaged in matters of the flesh…'

'Yes, that's right!' Amy retorted. 'When he lies with me, he also likes to beat me!'

Thomas's face lost its colour, and he gasped in horror. 'If this was his normal behaviour, why did you remain with him, and why have you only now decided to flee?'

With a bitter laugh she threw open the blanket, to reveal a heavily swollen belly.

'You are with child?' he gasped.

'Yes, I'm carrying the brute's seed inside me, and I fear for its safety if I stay with him. For all I know it'll be the Devil's own spawn, but while it's in my belly I've got to protect it.'

'So you will not return to your husband?'

'Would you, in my place? Of course you wouldn't, so it looks as if I need to ask the Brewsters to take me back.'

'Will your husband not come looking for you?'

'Only when he wants something from me, but I was hoping you'd be there to protect me from him.'

'But I abide here, and women are not allowed inside,' Thomas explained.

Amy cast a disparaging look up at the building behind him and snorted. 'I can't imagine any woman *wanting* to go inside there. You'd better return to living with Master Brewster.'

'You ask a lot of me.'

'I won't be ungrateful, and if you don't want to beat me I can always find ways to reward you.'

'While you remain a married woman? You wish to lead me into sin?'

'No, but I want you to take me back to the Brewster house. At least there I won't be ridden and walloped by a brute full of liquor.'

Thomas was powerless to resist her plea. By sunset that day, Amy was installed in the schuilkerken in exchange for general domestic duties, while Thomas secured Brewster's permission for him to take up residence in what had once been a wood store in the small yard to the rear of the premises. Each day he walked back and forth to his work in the Oosterdok, and now it was his entire income that was handed over for the general use of the congregation and its founder.

In the autumn of 1609 Amy gave birth to a daughter, whom she named Joanna. She had been assisted in what proved to be a straightforward childbirth by Mary Brewster, and she had been back on her feet for several weeks when she received an unwanted visitor.

It was very early in the morning, and Amy was drawing water from the well at the rear of the premises. Thomas was watching over her while he pulled on his boots, ready for his morning walk to his labours. Suddenly, an angry shout broke the silence, and a man stormed into the yard via the side entrance, bearing down on Amy.

'*Vrouw, kom hier!*' he yelled, and Thomas walked across the yard to intercept him.

'My husband!' Amy gasped.

Thomas stepped in front of the newcomer with an angry glare. 'If you are indeed the foul wretch who so badly used this innocent young woman, then even though you are married in the sight of God, I shall resist any effort on your part to reclaim her. Go back to wherever you came from.'

'*Ze heeft mijn baby!*' the man shouted back, and there was at least one word in that sentence that Thomas recognised.

'You lost all claim to any child when you beat her mother, thereby placing both their lives in danger!' Thomas yelled back.

'Have a care, Thomas,' came a voice behind him, and he turned to see William Bradford standing at the rear door.

'It is *he* who should have a care!' Thomas shouted as he jerked his head towards de Kuyper. 'If he comes one step closer to Amy, I'll knock him to the ground!'

'That's not what I meant,' Bradford replied. 'I have no doubt that you could plant him in the mud, but his family is one of the most powerful in Amsterdam.'

'No family is more powerful than one gathered in God's name,' Thomas retorted, still white with rage, 'so just let him move one step further, and I'll prove it!'

Fortunately for all concerned, de Kuyper had one trait possessed by all bullies — he was a coward. After eyeing Thomas up and down and recognising his slim chances of prevailing against him, he turned on his heel and stormed out of the yard, hurling what sounded like obscenities in Thomas's direction.

Amy scuttled up to Thomas, threw her arms around him and kissed him warmly on the lips. 'That's from both me *and* Joanna,' she whispered huskily as she retrieved her bucket, filled it and hurried back inside the house, walking past Bradford in the doorway. 'God certainly has a strong arm to protect us all from evil,' she added.

Bradford smiled sadly at Thomas. 'Let's hope he protects us from the de Kuyper family,' he remarked as he followed Amy back inside.

The import of his words became obvious the following day, when soldiers arrived, intent on taking Thomas into custody on a charge of abducting Amy and holding her and her child against her will. Fortunately, Bradford had taken the time to learn Dutch, and the men were sent away when he explained the full circumstances to them. He assured them that if they wanted to take the matter further, then they would find themselves prosecuting Arnoud de Kuyper for vicious assaults on his own wife.

But it was more than coincidence that the schuilkerken came under closer scrutiny from the civic authorities almost immediately thereafter. They were also given notice that the annual rent was set to rise by an unconscionable amount when its current period ran out. A town official came to visit and advised them that the neighbouring town of Leiden would welcome them, provided they undertook to obey its laws, and that William Brewster would be offered a more permanent position within its university if he were a citizen of that town.

After congregation meetings and fervent prayers for guidance, the entire community endured yet another move, in the hope that better times lay ahead in Leiden.

By this time the congregation had risen to thirty or so, including the children, who were not admitted to the meetings until they came of age. They could no longer rely on the old ways, when Master Brewster, lord of the manor, would play host to the meetings in his own home. Their new unspoken leader was William Bradford, an orphan from originally wealthy farming stock, and it was he who organised the roster of houses in their latest town. Alongside him, as ever, was the faithful and clean-living Thomas Bailey, who was still valued more for his physical strength than his religious fervour or depth of learning.

He was certainly highly valued by Amy, who treated him with the same regard that she would a husband, although she eventually gave up the hopeless campaign to overcome his moral scruples in order to entice him into her bed. She could accept that she was destined never to have the comfort of a husband, but she was determined that her daughter Joanna would not grow up without a father. She rarely missed an opportunity to persuade Thomas to hold the infant in his arms while she set about some domestic task, and those who called on the Brewsters soon became familiar with the sight of baby Joanna nestled in Thomas's burly arms while Amy fussed around the two of them. It was Thomas who assisted in the simple tasks of changing Joanna's soiled linen, comforting her to sleep when she was teething, and, as she grew older, watching carefully as she pushed herself upright then made the dash towards his outstretched arms, as he cried with delight at her first steps.

Her first word was 'Dadda', since this was the one that Amy used most often when encouraging her to speak. By age three it had become 'Dadda Tom', and 'Dadda Tom' it would remain throughout her childhood.

Thomas, for his part, was besotted, and if anyone had been unwise enough to challenge his role as the father figure in Joanna's life, he would have found himself lying flat in the dust. Little Joanna's beauty flourished as she reached double figures, and Thomas lovingly watched her grow, indulging her in almost every wish.

9

William Bradford had inherited a small fortune from his grandfather when he came of age in 1611.

His first action had been to establish his own fustian business in a substantial house in Leiden, and his second was to repay the kindness of his benefactor and surrogate father. When they had first settled in Leiden, given their financial distress, the Brewsters, along with Amy, Thomas and little Joanna, had been obliged to take up residence in a ramshackle hovel on a street known as the Stincksteeg. Bradford now insisted on relocating the Brewsters to a fine old house close to the magnificent local church building known as Pieterskerk.

He also purchased much land around it, until the church was surrounded by small cottages, each occupied by a congregation member and their family, and collectively known as the Green Close. One of these was allocated to Thomas, who was engaged as the general handyman for the community. Amy remained within the Brewster house, performing general household duties, although during her rare off-duty hours she could be found in or around Thomas's cottage, smiling complacently and watching the interaction between Thomas and Joanna.

By 1615 the congregation that met for compulsory worship had risen to over forty, with the men seated down one side of the large chapel, and women down the other. It was no less fervent in its worship, and it was left alone by the civic authorities, who were only too grateful to have in their midst an academic inspiration such as Pastor John Robinson, who taught at Leiden University, and William Brewster, a lecturer who was also an experienced printer of religious tracts in the English language.

As Brewster's fame as a printer began to spread beyond Leiden, he was able to found and finance his own press. Ever one for spreading his own beliefs, he was soon authoring pamphlets containing Separatist doctrines, which were smuggled into England in the false bottoms of wine barrels. John Robinson and Brewster's printing partner, Edward Winslow, were also contributors to the documents.

William Bradford made regular voyages across the North Sea, ostensibly selling his corduroy products, but also in order to ensure that the pamphlets printed by Brewster were not detected until they had reached their destination. During such trips, he would reside in a lodging house in Aldgate that was patronised by sea captains. From them he learned much regarding the comings and goings of merchant vessels, their types and capabilities, and the foreign ports to which they set sail, which increasingly included newly founded English colonies in the Americas, financed by London merchants.

Not long after he began his trips to London, Bradford was asked by a wealthy London textile merchant called Thomas May to bring back news of his brother, who had settled with his wife and daughter in Amsterdam. His generosity in doing so was well rewarded when he met the man's niece, a young lady called Dorothy May, who in 1613 became Mistress Bradford.

Things might have continued in this comfortable vein forever, had not William Brewster and Edward Winslow overreached themselves in their enthusiasm to draw attention to the extent to which the English King James was taking his Church of England down the road to perdition while seeking to put an end to the presbyteries in Scotland. They published a pamphlet entitled *Perth Assembly*, described by the monarch whose religious policies it attacked as an 'atrocious and seditious libel'.

King James immediately ordered the English Ambassador to the Low Countries to arrest Brewster and bring him to justice in England. Fortunately for him, Brewster was too well regarded by the authorities in Holland, and they politely declined the English request to hand him over. However, it was clear that the community he was part of was now in danger. When a power struggle within the Netherlands resulted in the execution of a home-grown Separatist called Johan van Oldenbarnevelt, the congregation's anxieties increased.

For almost eighty years Holland had been at war with Spain, whose forces had overrun the Low Countries in a previous generation. It had been the English Queen Elizabeth's support for the Dutch that had finally provoked Philip of Spain to launch his Armada at England, and when it failed ignominiously he had found it advantageous to forge a peace treaty with the Dutch. This was due to expire in 1621, and all Separatists feared that a Spanish re-conquest would bring with it an Inquisition designed to exterminate all but followers of the Catholic faith. The Leiden congregation could expect no leniency in that regard, and those who gathered for worship under the spiritual guidance of John Robinson muttered fearfully regarding what they could expect if Spain once again ruled Holland.

Rather than combining their followers into a united resistance against the common enemy, the two leaders of the rival factions within the Low Countries Council fell out radically over religious doctrine. The titular ruler, Prince Maurice of Orange, was a die-hard Calvinist, whereas his Chief Minister van Oldenbarnevelt was of a more Separatist persuasion. When the latter was executed for alleged 'subversion' that was generally held to have been a convenient invention, beneath which was a thinly veiled power struggle, the remaining Separatists within the Dutch Republic felt themselves to be somehow under suspicion.

When Prince Maurice looked towards England for support against a feared Spanish invasion, one of the prices demanded by King James was the persecution, if not the actual handing over, of Brewster the radical publisher. It was a red-faced mayor of Leiden who, late one afternoon, advised Brewster that he had been ordered by Prince Maurice to close down the printing press whose output had so incensed the English king. William Bradford had been acting as interpreter and seemed strangely unmoved by what sounded like a major disaster for the congregation in Leiden. Once the door had closed behind the mayor, and a stern-faced Thomas had escorted the mayoral party out of the Green Close, Bradford turned to Brewster with a smile.

'It would clearly not be in our long-term interests to remain here, but fortunately I am able to suggest an alternative, as the result of my many trips to England in recent times.'

'Not a return to England?' Brewster asked in a voice laden with dread.

Bradford shook his head with a smile. 'No. I have in mind a new land, where there is no king, no Parliament, and no established Church. A land in which we would be free to govern ourselves as a community, establish our own religion and dictate our own destinies.'

'Does such a land exist?'

'Indeed it does. It is called "the Americas" — or, as some call it, "the New World".'

'I have obviously heard of it,' Brewster conceded, 'but it lies far across the ocean, does it not? How do you propose that we get there? Have we the resources to establish a new nation among the native tribes and unyielding soil?'

'I cannot speak for either the native tribes or the soil,' Bradford conceded, 'but as for the rest, it can be done as a partnership with a body of merchants whose acquaintance I have made in London. They call themselves the Merchant Adventurers, and they seek to profit from the riches to be brought back from the New World. They have the finance for ships, equipment, crops and weapons. What they lack are willing volunteers to hazard their lives in such a venture. Therefore they would, I feel sure, be open to such overtures as we might make to them, as a group seeking the freedom to found an English colony for religious reasons. We will then repay the investment with shipments back to London of any material riches that are to be found there.'

Brewster fixed Bradford with a stern gaze. 'It is not just you and I we must consider here, William. Nor can we take it upon ourselves to inflict such upheaval on those who join with us in worship. It must be debated in a meeting, and the majority must prevail. But you should first return to London in order to confirm that there are those there who would finance such a venture.'

Bradford agreed, since he had already begun to make the necessary contacts. Apart from his own wide circle of sea captains, he had been introduced to a merchant called Thomas Weston, a Londoner reputed to have many business associates interested in exploring the Americas without actually hazarding their own welfare in the process. Weston had an agent in Holland already, a man called Edward Pickering who had married a Leiden woman with Separatist beliefs, and who was barely a nudge away from becoming a member of the eager congregation that met in the Green Close.

There was an even closer connection between John Robinson and another man who could negotiate on behalf of the Separatists with London merchants. John Carver had made his way over to Holland some years previously, and had there met, and fallen for, Katherine White. Katherine was the sister of Bridget White, whom John Robinson had married back in England. Carver and Robinson were therefore brothers-in-law, and once it became known that Carver had not only business experience but also merchant contacts in London, he and William Bradford acted as agents for the Leiden congregation. In the process they recruited a man called Robert Cushman, another refugee in Leiden with a history of persecution for his Separatist views. Between them they proved to be astute negotiators, once the congregation that they represented agreed overwhelmingly that the time was ripe for one more transfer to another place.

They were assisted considerably by the fact that King James had proved as enthusiastic as his predecessor Queen Elizabeth to settle and plunder the land on the eastern shores of the Americas. To this end he had sponsored two joint-stock companies to colonise the area: the Virginia Company and the Plymouth Company.

By the time that Carver and Cushman approached Thomas Weston, the Virginia Company had already established the Jamestown Settlement in the southern half of the territory. However, it was struggling after failing to find the anticipated gold beneath its surface, and by 1617 there had been no volunteers for the northern half. The interest now being shown by a somewhat naive group of religious zealots based in Holland revived hopes that perhaps the land between the

Chesapeake Bay and the Canadian border might be exploited, and serious negotiations began.

The reality was that the coalition of London merchants that Weston had put together were interested only in the profits to be made from the importation into England of whatever resources the land might yield. It had long been recognised that exploitation of the land required human effort, which in turn required the establishment of a colony of willing workers. The merchants were not prepared to uproot themselves from their comfortable urban lifestyles and engage in manual labour, so an expression of interest from a group of volunteers seeking a place in which to worship God in their own way was too good to dismiss. Furthermore, experience had shown that Puritan types included hard labour among their virtues, so Separatists seemed ideal for the task.

When Bradford reported back to Leiden that he had managed to organise a passage to the New World for the Leiden congregation, there were very few opposed to accepting the challenge. Over thirty of the congregation began packing their few humble possessions, and the Green Close was soon buzzing with anticipation.

Thomas, as a member of the congregation, had raised his hand in favour of the move, but those of his fellow worshippers who employed servants merely assumed that they would also be making the journey. Indeed, very few of the domestic staff wished to be left behind in a dour little township in which they had no family connections, and whose language they didn't speak, and Amy was no different from the rest. One evening, while Thomas was sweeping the yard behind the Meeting Room, she sent little Joanna scurrying out, carrying a freshly baked loaf.

'Dadda Tom, here's your tea from Mamma!' she lisped as she ran towards him, and he threw down his brush to lift her off her feet and swing her round in a circle.

Amy appeared in the doorway as usual. 'Would you miss us, if you were to go on a ship away from here, leaving us to fend for ourselves?'

'I would, but is not Master Brewster taking you both with him?'

'He hasn't said so. But if not, can't we go with you? After all, you *are* Joanna's father, after a fashion.'

'I'm her father *whatever* the fashion,' Thomas insisted proudly, 'but if you do not travel as a servant to the Brewsters, then you can hardly come as my wife, can you?'

'But if we go far away from here,' Amy argued, 'then we'll never know if de Kuyper dies, leaving me free to marry you. So what's to be done?'

'Think not of marriage,' Thomas reminded her yet again, 'but leave it to me to remind Master Brewster that we would be lost to starvation without your excellent stews and loafs. I am reminded of the story of the loaves and fishes whenever we sit down to one of your wholesome meals.'

The following day, a chastened William Brewster apologised to Amy for not having formally invited her to continue in his service, since he had simply assumed that she would be content to travel as part of the household. She gleefully consented and sent Joanna in search of Thomas in order to give him a big kiss and thank him for his kindness.

Word came from Bradford, who was back in London, that the final supplies were being assembled, and that a vessel called the *Speedwell* would moor in the nearby port of Delfshaven in July. It would transport the congregation across the Channel to the English port of Southampton, where they would join a larger vessel called the *Mayflower*. The *Mayflower* had been commissioned in London in order to cross the Atlantic in convoy with the *Speedwell*, and it would be carrying the remaining colonists.

On 22nd July 1620, the sixty-ton pinnace cast off and began to creak its way downriver from the inland port. From the quayside, Pastor Robinson boomed out a prayer for God's guidance and protection in the new life that the thirty-five Separatists from Leiden were seeking.

10

'How can you know that it won't sink to the bottom?' a terrified Joanna asked Thomas for the fifth time as she clung to him. They were in the comparatively shallow waters off the French coast as the captain opted to take advantage of the wind gauge before hazarding the dash north into Southampton. The *Speedwell* was bucking, both from side to side and up and down, and Joanna's face was green as she watched her mother vomiting over the gunnels.

'Because this is how ships work,' Thomas reassured Joanna. 'They float on the water, which is why we are moving up and down in the manner that Mamma finds not to her liking. It is because the ship is able to move in this fashion, on the surface, that we can be assured that we shall not sink.'

'I think I might welcome that,' Amy groaned as she heaved yet again.

Joanna looked away. 'How much longer will this go on, Dadda?' she asked.

Thomas called across to a deckhand who was busily coiling ropes under the poop. 'How soon before we reach harbour again?' he asked.

The deckhand walked over, shaking his head. 'Depends on the wind, doesn't it? But she's wallowing on account of all the water she's shipped, so that'll slow her down a bit. Sometime tomorrow, maybe, but who knows?'

Thomas looked up and down the deck. 'I can't see all that much water on deck, and most of it seems to swill back out through the sides in between waves.'

'I wasn't talking about water up top,' the deckhand muttered as he walked closer. 'She's taking in half the bloody ocean down below in her main hold. It doesn't seem to matter how often we caulk her, because the timbers are too old, and they've taken to shrinking.'

'If she's leaking below decks,' Thomas whispered back, hoping that Joanna was too concerned about her mother to pay much attention, 'how will she make it across to the Americas?'

'Damned if I know,' the deckhand replied as he spat on the deck, 'but I can tell you this much — she won't have me aboard when she tries.'

'Ah, there you are!' called a confident voice.

Thomas smiled as he turned to see William Bradford approaching from the bow. He was dodging the spray alongside Myles Standish, a stocky little man whom Thomas had been attempting to keep his distance from ever since he'd made his first appearance in their community. As a man of peaceful inclinations, unless roused to justified anger, Thomas had no time for so-called military men, and Standish seemed to be too eager to talk about matters of warfare. He constantly boasted about his days in the army of Queen Elizabeth, which had helped the Dutch to defend their territory against the Spanish. Even though Standish had subsequently become a friend of Pastor Robinson, Thomas was wary of him. If he was honest with himself, he had also felt resentful when Standish had been hired as the military adviser to the colony that was to be founded in the New World.

However, Thomas smiled weakly as the two men approached him, and Joanna moved down the deck to comfort her mother. He nodded ruefully at Amy and asked, 'How are your womenfolk managing in these heaving conditions?'

'I swear that Rose has thrown up more than she's consumed since we left Leiden,' said Standish.

'Dorothy's not much better,' Bradford added, 'although she's up front there, trying to persuade Rose that she's not about to die.'

'I'm advised that it will be tomorrow before we reach Southampton,' Thomas observed. 'At least then we'll get a respite from all this, but I dread to think how we'll survive once we head for the Americas. They say that there's much more ocean involved than a mere Channel crossing, and that it will be autumn before we get there.'

'If we get there at all,' Standish observed. 'As a fighting man in Her Majesty's army, I've made many crossings of the Channel, but never in a bucket as ill-disposed to the swell as this one.'

'That's why we came over, Thomas,' Bradford told him, 'since we seek your support in a change of plan.'

'Why should you be considering a change so early in our expedition?' Thomas asked. 'And is it not a matter that should be put to the congregation in meeting?'

'It's a matter that concerns our continued existence,' Bradford countered, 'and as one who feels keenly the responsibility of having persuaded so many of our brethren to embark on this voyage, I'm close to proposing that we do not hazard the main crossing in this old hulk. They tell me that she takes in water, and that cannot be good for a vessel about to cross the biggest ocean in the world.'

'I believe that Captain Drake proved that the Atlantic is not the largest ocean some years ago,' Standish corrected him, 'but your point is well made. I agree with William's proposal that we seek passage on the larger vessel — the *Mayflower* — that will be joining us at Southampton with the other colonists.'

Thomas was surprised. 'I was not aware that we had a choice of vessel,' he replied. 'As I understand matters, we are to travel on this one, and the other is reserved for other colonists who have booked their passage directly from London.'

'The *Mayflower* is intended to transport others in the venture, certainly,' Bradford agreed, 'but they are, in the main, either those who have paid for a passage, or those sent by our financiers to protect their investment. Either way, they are not dedicated to God's ways in the same manner as we are.'

'And they're therefore less likely to entrust their lives to an old wreck of a vessel like this, in the belief that God will preserve them for their piety and devotion,' Thomas observed. 'I suspect that they could not be persuaded to change places with us.'

When they limped into Southampton, the *Mayflower* was already moored in the Inner Sound and had taken on board only fresh fruit and water. She had aboard some sixty-five paying passengers, many of whom had sunk their meagre life savings into the prospect of growing rich on the other side of the world and returning to enjoy a higher social standing in England. In the main they were middle-class traders and craftsmen such as millers, farriers, bakers and farmers. Below decks were the many provisions that their sponsors had insisted they would need in order to forge a new existence in a hostile land. In addition to food, tools and medicines there were also some animals, and a consignment of cannon, shot and gunpowder with which to defend themselves against any natives they might encounter, not to mention those from other explorer nations who might resent competition for the spoils of the Americas.

When negotiations to transfer the Separatist party to the *Mayflower* proved fruitless, Bradford insisted that the *Speedwell* be thoroughly re-caulked, and in places re-planked completely. This resulted in a month's delay, during which both communities were fed and watered from the supplies that had been loaded into the holds of the *Mayflower* for the journey to the Americas. There was a good deal of muttering from all quarters regarding the delay, since autumn in the Atlantic normally brought with it heavy gales that blew from the west, meaning that westbound vessels had to engage in lengthy tacking manoeuvres that were both time-consuming and uncomfortable for passengers.

It was obvious even from a distance that the *Mayflower* was in all ways a far superior vessel to the *Speedwell*. She was much longer, at ninety feet, and her storage capacity was almost triple that of the smaller vessel. She was also carrying more passengers, some sixty-five in number, and they had paid for their passage. The merchant company that had funded the entire enterprise was therefore hardly likely to agree to allow the thirty or so Separatists on board, for they had nothing to offer at this stage but their religious fervour.

After the month-long delay for repairs to the *Speedwell*, the two vessels departed Southampton. However, late on the second day, they were obliged to put into Dartmouth for further work on the *Speedwell*, which was once again leaking to such a degree that her master refused to proceed into the open Atlantic. Almost two weeks later, there was a cheer from those lining the decks of the *Mayflower* as they drifted past Land's End. But when the *Speedwell* sprang a leak the following day, the two vessels were forced to retrace their course for two hundred miles back into Plymouth. Once they had arrived, the God-fearing passengers on board the *Speedwell* refused to travel another nautical mile in her, unless it was back to Holland.

The master and part owner of the *Mayflower*, Christopher Jones, was now obliged to make an executive decision on behalf of those who had chartered the vessel for the voyage to the New World. If he obliged the Separatist party from Leiden to remain on the *Speedwell* and hazard an Atlantic crossing during the autumn westerly gales, he would almost certainly be condemning them to their deaths. Although not a deeply religious man, he possessed the superstitious nature of all seadogs, and he was uneasy about such a prospect. If, on the other hand, he allowed them on board the *Mayflower*, he would be stretching both the accommodation and the provisions allocated to the original party of sixty-five who had boarded the vessel in Blackwall. But his charterers would reward him with additional payment for the extra passengers, and possibly future charters.

It was eventually William Bradford who persuaded him that it was his Christian duty not to turn his back on his fellow men and women. With some misgivings Captain Jones gave approval for the transfer, and in the first week of September 1620, the *Mayflower* slipped its moorings in Plymouth carrying a total of 102 passengers and over thirty crew.

Conditions would have been harsh enough even in good weather. The *Mayflower* had been constructed for cargo transport and had previously specialised in the transfer of wine and textiles across the Channel. As a result, she was not built for passenger transport, and the charterers had not insisted that she be refitted for that purpose. The bulk of the passengers were therefore consigned to what had been designed originally as a gun deck, a space measuring fifty feet by twenty-five feet, with a low ceiling and side ports through which cannon could protrude, but which allowed the ocean to cascade in during stormy weather. There was no privy, and passengers were required to make use of such buckets as they might find.

Below them was the cargo hold, with its constantly shifting load of personal possessions, tools, weapons and spare clothing. There was no purpose-built companionway to allow access from the gun deck to the fresh air of the main deck, and anyone seeking to access it was required to hazard life and limb on a rope ladder. This might have been adequate for mariners experienced in its use, but it was hardly welcoming to farmers, merchants and pilgrims dressed in breeches, boots, coats or long gowns. The passengers forced to occupy this accommodation eyed with envy the narrow area under the forecastle where the deckhands huddled to sleep when not on duty. The captain's cabin, meanwhile, was at the top of the aftercastle, which rose to a height of some thirty feet. This structure was an additional hazard in high winds, due to its tendency to catch the gale and make the vessel much more top-heavy.

There was no shortage of gales once they ventured out beyond the relative shelter of England's Western Approaches. It was now mid-autumn, and the howling wind blew from the west. The necessity to make long tacks to the north and south in order to make forward progress meant that once the passengers had acclimatised themselves to lurching to one side, they were then required to brace themselves in the opposite direction. Below decks was soon a sea of vomit that not even the deckhands would venture down into, and such food as it was possible to prepare in the forecastle was routinely refused by those who knew that it would only come back up again within the hour.

Predictably, Amy Tasker was one of the first to succumb to seasickness. Thomas and Joanna spent days on end holding her upright while she threw up right and left, apologising all the time to the nearest fellow passengers, who were in no better condition themselves. She refused to eat, and as she grew weaker she took to shivering uncontrollably. She was not the only one below decks to do so, and at first it was believed that the cause of the collective distress was the occasional cascade of seawater through the gaps in the closed gun ports. Then the first death occurred, and those on board with experience in such matters declared it to have been the result of pneumonia.

There were soon a handful of corpses below decks, and those who remained alive had to make the heartrending choice of how to dispose of them. They were still, by the captain's calculation, at least a week out from landfall across the ocean, and there was only one form of burial known at sea. Since John Robinson was one of those who had been left behind, it was the ageing William Brewster who led the prayers that accompanied the respectful lowering of the dead into the waves. Further prayers were said for the preservation of those who remained as the saddened company sloshed back down into the passenger compartment.

Thomas and Joanna still sat on either side of Amy, who was icy to the touch and soaked to the skin.

Joanna looked across at Thomas with tears in her eyes. 'What can we do, Dadda?' she asked. 'Mamma is so cold, like she's already dead. Can we not find some way to warm her?'

Joanna was herself soaked to the skin, having thrown herself over her mother every time more water barrelled in from the leaky gun port above them. Thomas reminded himself that this was no duty for an eleven-year-old girl to be called upon to perform, but her actions had given him an idea.

'Perhaps we can give her our own warmth?' he suggested. They wrapped their arms around each other and lay across as much of Amy's torso as they could. There was something so comforting and peaceful about what they were doing that Thomas felt his head beginning to nod, and a few seconds later he was asleep, exhausted after days of ministering to Amy. When he awoke, it was to the sound of someone calling his name feebly from a distance, and with a joyous start he recognised Amy's voice. He sat up, and she was smiling up at him, conscious for the first time in days.

'You never did get to make me Mistress Bailey,' she whispered hoarsely, 'and now it's too late. But you must promise to look after our daughter — to defend her with your life, if need be. Mine's all but over, but we may meet together in the hereafter, if Pastor Robinson was telling the truth all these years.'

'No talk of death,' Thomas urged her.

'There's nothing else ahead of me, but you must promise. She's more your daughter than if you'd seeded her yourself, so promise me.'

'Of course I promise,' Thomas reassured her. 'But you must rest.'

'So must you,' she insisted.

Thomas laid his head next to her and allowed the tears to flow freely. Further sleep spared him the agony of hearing her final breath. When he awoke again, it was to the gentle urging of Joanna as she tugged at his sleeve.

'Dadda, there's a voice on deck telling us that we've finally sighted land.'

11

Thomas fought his way up the rope ladder, blinded by his tears but anxious to see land at long last. On the starboard side of the heaving vessel, he found Brewster and Bradford deep in conversation with Standish, and he made his way carefully over the deck in order to give them the awful tidings.

'Amy just died,' he choked out.

Bradford placed a comforting arm across his shoulder. 'She was precious to you, I know, even though you never married. How is your daughter?'

'I left Joanna sobbing bitterly over her mother's body; it was she who advised me that we have sighted land.'

'So we have, such as it is,' Standish observed. He pointed through the spray at a grey line on which waves could be seen breaking heavily.

'Is that where we have been heading these past months?' Thomas asked.

Brewster shook his head. 'It seems that we are too far north. Our charter gave us land to a northernmost limit of forty-one degrees latitude, but Captain Jones calculates that whatever this land is, it lies at least a degree to the north of that limit.'

'So will he turn the vessel round and head further south?'

Bradford and Standish exchanged uneasy glances before Bradford supplied an answer. 'Therein lies a difficulty. The wind drives us from the southwest, and given the state of the ship, and the number of those who have died, he is disinclined to turn her head into a howling gale. He proposes that we search for a safe landing point and await a change in the weather, and only then head south.'

'By which time, how many more will have died?' Thomas demanded angrily.

Bradford nodded. 'That was also my response, but Captain Jones is adamant. He reminds us that this is his vessel, and he is responsible for her.'

'He is also responsible for the remaining human lives aboard her!' Thomas protested. 'How many more must die?'

'Softly, Thomas,' Brewster urged him. 'I understand your anger, given the recent loss of Amy, but we must step back a pace and consider what is best for the venture long term. We have no right to step ashore where we are now, since it is not part of the land that was given to us in the charter from the Virginia Company. Logic dictates that we do as the captain orders: await better weather, then make our way south.'

'And how much have we left in provisions?' Standish challenged him.

Brewster's face fell. 'Precious little, I am advised. Much of it has rotted due to the constant drenching it has received these many weeks, and we were fortunate that so many of those below decks declined to eat when the sickness overtook them, else we would by now be in a state of starvation.'

'A good argument for venturing ashore,' Standish urged them. 'I need to dry out some of the powder and balls we brought with us, and then I can lead a party ashore to shoot something we can feed to our fellow travellers.'

Brewster sighed. 'By the look of that barren scrub in the distance, there would be precious little in the way of a target for your slaughter. In any case, we must abide by whatever the captain decides. And Thomas's sad news reminds us that there are several more sea burials to be organised.'

Later that day, Amy's body was dropped into the water. Thomas held Joanna close, and her wails were muffled by his cloak. Eventually, when the mourners had tactfully withdrawn below decks, she raised a tear-stained face and asked, 'Will you continue to look after me, even though Mamma has gone?'

Thomas smiled down kindly and kissed the top of her bonneted head. 'Why would I not? You're my daughter, after all.'

Joanna paused. 'You're not my real father, are you?'

'And how does one judge a real father?' Thomas teased her. 'You were not from my loins, certainly, but I am the only father you have known. Would you reject me now, after all that we have shared?'

'No!' she protested. 'I just wished to be sure that now that Mamma has gone, you will at least see to my welfare. I have no claim on you.'

'Your claim on me is the love that binds us together,' Thomas told her as tears began to form in his eyes. 'I could have claimed your mother as my life partner, should I have wished, but she was still married to the man who was your real father, and that would have been a sin. But from the day I first set eyes on you, I have loved you like a daughter. If you love me as I love you, then give me your hand and let us continue in this new life as father and daughter.'

Two days later, Captain Jones invited Brewster and John Carver into his cabin, along with two representatives of those who had travelled west in search of fortune. It was agreed that they would continue north alongside the long strip of land, then turn into what they hoped would prove to be a broad bay, in which they could seek shelter from the Atlantic gale that had dogged their entire voyage. There they would drop anchor and a party of men would venture ashore in search of food. When the weather proved more clement, they would venture back out into the open ocean and set a course south for the river that had been named 'Hudson' by earlier explorers, where they had been authorised to settle the land in the name of King James.

A ragged cheer broke out from those on deck looking eagerly landward as the tip of the long promontory came in sight, and the *Mayflower* was steered into calmer waters on its leeward side. Captain Jones ordered the dropping of the anchor, and clouds of dust ascended into the swirling wind as the ropes and chains were deployed for the first time in sixty-six days. It had stopped raining, and Standish appeared on deck with a triumphant grin, carrying a bundle of objects covered by a coarse cloth.

'Who will join me ashore?' he called out.

John Carver stepped forward. Although he had been one of those negotiating on behalf of the Leiden congregation for their inclusion in the overall expedition, he had become a voice for those on board who were more interested in making their fortune. 'I will go with you gladly,' he announced, 'in order that I may lay claim to such riches as may be found there, on behalf of those who have appointed me as their spokesman.'

Brewster nudged Thomas's elbow. 'You should go too, Thomas,' he urged him in a low voice. 'It is important that we pilgrims be among those who first step ashore, and I fear that Myles Standish may be too arrogant and aggressive towards any native tribes that he may encounter. We cannot afford to begin our new life at war with natives.'

'There are natives out there?' Joanna asked fearfully as she looked up at Thomas. 'Have a care, Father.'

Thomas smiled down at her. 'You wish to eat something more wholesome than the sodden ruins of provisions? If so, then I must obtain such.'

'Do you know how to fire a musket?' Standish challenged him.

'No, but you can teach me,' Thomas replied confidently. 'If it comes to that, know you how to launch a spear or fire an arrow? My father was a carpenter and a woodsman, and he taught me how to bring birds down from trees and spear rabbits.'

'I will go also,' Jonathan Brewster chimed in as he stepped forward. 'Thomas taught me his skills back in England, and I provided for the pot each day.'

'Please keep a watchful eye on him, Thomas,' William Brewster muttered.

Thomas nodded. 'I promise I will.' Jonathan may have attained his twenty-seventh year, but his common sense was still lacking. Much though Thomas disliked the young man's enduring pomposity and self-importance, he would not wish to see him come to any harm.

The shallop lashed to the inner timbers of the poop was now untied, lowered into the waters and held steady by the ship's four crew members who were to row it ashore as part of the landing party. After thirty minutes of hard pulling against an outgoing tide, the bow crunched onto a gravelly beach, and Myles Standish was the first to set foot on this new colonial territory. He turned round, holding his musket high above his head. 'Come, my brave friends, and let us see what form our supper tonight shall take!' he called to the others. They followed him with some trepidation, looking out for natives who might object to this invasion of their territory.

They saw none, but encountered much evidence that they had been there, and probably recently. Standish, who claimed to have been trained to track enemy soldiers in retreat, pointed out several patches of blackened earth where fires had burned, and abandoned piles of stones that might once have been the lower levels of crude shelters. But it was Thomas who recognised something unusual about what at a cursory glance might have been mistaken for a wood pile. He had never before encountered a timber stack with an animal hide for a cover, and when he saw three such structures in a row, he drew Standish's attention to them, then lifted one of the covers out of curiosity. He smelled raw vegetation, and he grinned as he called out, 'At least they left us some corn!'

Standish hurried over, gave a cheer, and called for the sailors to fill the sacks they had brought with them with the corn that had obviously been left by local natives for winter provisions. Thomas looked nervously back into the line of trees behind them, searching for angry faces, but there were none. Then he saw Standish staring at the shore, where a straggler from the shallop had pulled a wriggling shape out of the water.

'Fish!' Standish yelled in triumph. 'Come, men, let us follow this proud fellow's example, and fill our sacks with God's abundance! When boiled down with this corn, the spoils of the day shall make a fine stew to warm us!'

An hour later, the shallop was creaking with the weight of a dozen sacks of fish and half a dozen sacks of corn. The men pulled back out of the shallows and returned to the *Mayflower* in triumph. They then eagerly handed the sacks up to the deckhands, and Standish stepped back on board.

'There is much fish to be had in the shallows out there!' he announced, as if he'd been the one to make the discovery.

The exhilaration was only temporary. After those who were in a condition to eat had consumed their fill of the fish and corn potage that several of the women had cooked under the supervision of Mary Brewster and Rose Standish, the depression settled back over the inhabitants of the *Mayflower* when it was announced that the following day they would raise anchor and sail back out into the roaring Atlantic. Once again, they would search for the more southerly land to which they were entitled under their charter.

The ferocity of the open ocean was plainly visible even from where they sat at anchor on the inner, western side of the narrow isthmus of land that curved back to the south. With shudders of dread, the passengers heard the anchor being raised with a rusty rattle, and the vessel seemed to jerk to life as it headed back towards the open ocean.

A week later, they were back where they had started, moored in the shelter of the bay and searching its curving shoreline for a suitable place to make a landing and build their first houses. They had spent the past seven days trying to force the vessel's bow south in the face of an intense low-pressure system that had driven a south-westerly tempest straight at them. They had travelled no more than a further twenty miles to the south before Captain Jones feared for the integrity of his craft if they continued to offer her beams as a target for mountainous seas, and he opted to turn the *Mayflower* around to ride that same wind swiftly back to the haven of the bay. The few passengers who were not rolling, throwing up or praying for deliverance gave a cheer as they recognised the change in the vessel's motion and acknowledged that there was a merciful God after all.

It was now midwinter, and through Captain Jones's eyeglass, the crew could see snow on the surrounding land. On the leeward side of the bay, the shoreline curved gently, and they could take their pick of where to land. However, since the *Mayflower* was now relatively still, and the only alternative was a wide stretch of land exposed to the elements, there was general agreement that until a township was available, with huts to protect them from the weather, daily life would continue on board the ship, whether or not landing parties were organised to venture ashore and build a township. And it was upon that point that opinion was divided.

For those who had ventured from Leiden, the precise location of where they took root in this new land was irrelevant. Anywhere would suffice for them to build huts, a new church and a fresh congregation under God's guidance and mercy. But the rest of the colonists had a different perspective. They had signed up in order to become the proud owners of a piece of land between certain degrees of Earth's latitude, and where they had dropped anchor was somewhat to the north of that. The muttered arguments between the two groups of voyagers grew louder and more aggressive regarding the legality of the bargain that had been entered into. William Brewster anxiously called Myles Standish, John Carver, William Bradford, Edward Winslow and Thomas to a hushed meeting under the forecastle.

'Gentlemen,' he began, 'we appear to be at risk of anarchy before we even step ashore. Those who joined our expedition in London, and are not fired by the love of God, think only of material gain. They are insisting that since we are not to be landed in any place that was covered by the contract they signed before venturing aboard, they are not bound by any pre-existing terms and conditions, but may simply step ashore and lay claim to whatsoever land they wish. Clearly, if they are allowed to leave this vessel on those terms, men will be slaughtering each other within hours.'

'We surely need to establish some sort of community, with laws,' Bradford agreed. 'But if we simply abide by the laws of England, do we not once again become a persecuted minority because of our manner of worship?'

110

'What other laws *are* there?' Thomas asked. 'And why am I called to this meeting?'

'At my request,' Standish told him. 'If there is to be law and order imposed, then I am the most qualified to administer it, and I see in you a worthy deputy. You have a strong arm, a sturdy courage and a stout heart. And you will become skilled with weapons, once I have taught you how to fire a musket.'

'I am no man's second,' Thomas flared, 'and I would challenge your right to employ weapons against others in accordance with a law that does not exist!'

'Softly, Thomas,' Brewster urged him. 'I grow too old for this bickering among young hotheads while we have issues of great import to resolve. You speak of a law that does not exist, which is why we are met. We must agree on a constitution by which this new land is to be governed, and then we shall be justified in enforcing that constitution, by force if necessary.'

Edward Winslow had thus far remained silent, but now he joined the conversation. 'There is a ready-made constitution in the land from which we all originate, even those of us who spent some years in Leiden. Its one failing was that it did not acknowledge the right of all men — and for that matter, women — to worship in accordance with their own conscience. I propose a loose statement of loyalty to a new colony under the English crown, with freedom of religion and conscience as its foundation.'

'And how do you propose that we make it binding?' Standish asked.

'If a man is so unworthy that his signature is not also his bond of honour, then we do not wish him to be part of our new community, surely?' Thomas suggested.

Carver smiled. 'Spoken like one who governs a nation already. Your point is a valid one, and I propose that we offer a

111

choice to those who remain on board here. They may join with us, under our governance, or they may choose to put ashore somewhere else, and continue their lives without rules, without conscience, and probably without even common decency.'

'You would banish them from our midst?' Thomas asked.

Standish nodded. 'What does our former King do to those who disobey, or challenge his right to rule? At best he banishes them from the realm, and at worst he cuts off their heads.'

'But we have turned our backs on all that, surely?' Brewster objected. 'Our whole point in coming to this desolate spot was to found a society under which the only ruler was God himself, working through a chosen leader.'

'Chosen by God, or chosen by the people?' Winslow asked.

Bradford was quick to supply the answer. 'We have fled from a land in which a king claimed to have been chosen by God. No man can claim that — it must be the peoples' choice.'

'Therein lies the fundamental problem,' Carver observed. 'What if the choice of the people be not that of the person best suited to govern? Shall the others be justified in overthrowing him?'

'There is one among us who would be the perfect choice of those who follow God's urging, but who also enjoys the respect of those whose reason for being here is to reap rich reward,' said Brewster. 'A man who bows his head to God, but who is skilled in matters of commerce. The man who just confirmed that whoever is chosen must act always in the best interests of those who elected him, so that he will not be overthrown by his own villainous abuse of power.'

All eyes turned to Carver, who raised his hands in protest. 'You cannot mean me, surely? I am not worthy.'

It fell silent until Thomas added, 'A man whose modesty shines through, and demonstrates his perfect fitness for the title of king, emperor, or whatever.'

'Governor only,' Carver insisted. 'If I am to preside over this new nation, then that is all that I shall call myself. And even that is more than I am worthy of.'

'Then "Governor" it shall be,' said Brewster. 'Are we all agreed?'

There were nods all round, and Carver shook his head. 'I am both humbled and terrified to have such an honour bestowed upon me, and I thank you for your trust. But I will need a Council of State to assist me in making the right decisions.'

Brewster shook his head. 'Governance shall be by the people in meetings, just as we have always governed our humble congregation before God. But we shall need a broad document of commitment, to which all men may put their hands.'

'I will undertake to draft it,' Carver volunteered, 'given my familiarity with commercial contracts, and the fact that I shall be governed by whatever constitution I write. But I will keep it broad and simple, in order that we may in future proceed according to conscience and common sense, rather than be trammelled by words.'

'I have seen your hand,' Bradford said kindly. 'Therefore, I shall write to your dictation. Let us get to work.'

12

Three days later, on 11th November 1620, Brewster, Carver, Standish and Bradford stood under the forecastle of the *Mayflower*. In front of them stood all those capable of negotiating their way up the rope ladder from the ship's hold, and it fell instantly silent as Brewster called for order.

'We have reached the day of decision!' Brewster announced as he held up the document that Bradford had completed an hour previously, to the satisfaction of the group who had been consulted on its contents. 'You may either go your own way, and be guided by your own consciences, alone but independent, or you may join with those of us who chose to make this perilous journey because we have faith in God. If you choose to be part of this new community, then you will be required to sign to that effect and will be sworn to obey its simple conditions. The decision is entirely yours, and each man present who has a wife and family will, by placing his signature on this document, be committing them also. It will be known as the "Mayflower Compact", and its terms are simple but ambitious. They are as follows.'

Brewster gripped the document firmly with both hands to preserve it from the stiff breeze that was blowing across the deck, and read out the terms in a determined voice.

'In the name of God, Amen. We, whose names are underwritten, the loyal subjects of our dread sovereign lord King James, by the grace of God, of Great Britain, France, and Ireland, King, Defender of the Faith, et cetera. Having undertaken for the glory of God, and advancement of the Christian faith, and the honour of our King and country, a voyage to plant the first colony in the northern parts of Virginia; Do by these presents, solemnly and mutually, in the presence of God and one another, covenant and combine ourselves together into a civil body politick, for our better ordering and preservation, and furtherance of the ends aforesaid: And by virtue hereof do enact, constitute, and frame, such just and equal laws, ordinances, acts, constitutions, and officers, from time to time, as shall be thought most meet and convenient for the general good of the colony; unto which we promise all due Submission and Obedience. In witness whereof we have hereunto subscribed our names the eleventh of November, in the reign of our sovereign lord King James, of England, France, and Ireland, the eighteenth, and of Scotland the fifty-fourth, *Anno Domini*, 1620.'

'Fine words,' came a voice from the back, 'but what do they mean?'

William Bradford stepped forward. 'They mean that when we step ashore, it shall be as an orderly, law-abiding and civilised society, and not a land-grabbing rabble. By signing, you commit yourself and your families to a peaceful future safe in the protecting arms of your friends and companions, joined together under God's holy ordinance for the benefit of all, the weak alongside the strong.'

'And who shall be our leaders?' called another doubting voice.

'That will be decided by those who sign this document,' said Brewster. 'Only those who sign shall have a voice in the governance of our new colony, because only those who sign will be entitled to its protection when we step ashore.'

'And if we choose to stay on this ship?' asked another.

'For the rest of your lives? Have sense, man!' exclaimed Standish. 'Sooner or later you must all step ashore, and we are offering you the chance to be the first to do so, in order to claim whatever natural riches may be discovered there. I for one cannot wait to step from this prison, but I will only do so as a civilised member of a well-ordered society. Now, what shall it be?'

Slowly a queue began to form, and within minutes a total of forty-one men had signed for themselves and their families. In the main they were the Separatists who had begun their life's journey at Scrooby, but there were also a few others whose original ambition had been the acquisition of riches, but who could sense that their only hope of survival was to combine their interests with the majority. There were a few who hadn't signed, and they withdrew into a sullen group, intent on demanding that they be landed somewhere else. However, the majority waited eagerly for the next announcement, and it came from Standish.

'Now that we have a community under the Mayflower Compact, we need a leader. I have spent most of my long military career assessing men for various purposes, including the ability to lead others, and I nominate John Carver to be our first leader, with the title of "Governor". Most of you know him to be an honest man, and one with a wide knowledge of the world and its ways. It was he who drafted the Compact you just signed, so what say you?'

For want of any other nomination, John Carver became the first governor of the community. As he thanked the assembled company for their faith in him, he raised an important question. 'What name shall we give to our new settlement?'

There were a few mutterings among those who had signed the Compact, and a few nods of agreement, before John Allerton, a mariner, called out, 'How about "Plymouth"? It's where we began this journey as a group, and it's symbolic of our joint ambitions.'

Carver looked around briefly. 'Any other suggestions?' When there were none, he announced, '"Plymouth" it shall be, then, and God bless our first decision as a settlement of like-minded people. Now to the matter of governance.'

'I thought you'd just become our governor?' Richard Warren, a merchant, called out.

Carver nodded. 'Indeed I did, with all humility, and that same humility impresses upon me that unless our new colony is to be ruled by a despot, we shall also need a governing council. I propose that we call them "selectors", and that they be selected every year by popular vote among those who have signed the Compact. Who shall be our first selectors?'

'How about he whose wisdom brought about the Compact?' Bradford suggested. 'We who came through Leiden owe everything to our grey-haired old sage William Brewster, and we look to him for spiritual guidance.'

'Aye, William Brewster!' came several shouts.

Carver scanned the eager faces. 'No-one has any objection? Then William Brewster, you are elected.'

'As my first action as a selector,' Brewster replied, 'I nominate Myles Standish, since we chose him to organise our physical protection. If he is to act as our military leader, then it is appropriate that he is among those who gives our new governor guidance in such matters.'

Standish was duly elected, and he in turn nominated William Bradford, as deputy to William Brewster in matters of religious observance. Bradford proudly took his place at the front, and several minutes later Edward Winslow, William White and Isaac Allerton had been added to the list. William Brewster led the group on deck in a prayer of thanksgiving for such an easy process, and the majority of those who had signed the Compact made their way below decks to tell the women and children what had been decided. The selectors moved to the comparative shelter of the poop overhang to avoid the cold wind that had suddenly sprung up, and held their first meeting.

'What must be our first actions?' Carver asked eagerly.

'We first must find a suitable spot to settle,' said Standish. 'There are many miles of shoreline to be seen from here, and we shall need to select a spot where we may build a harbour. Adjoining that harbour we must build houses, so that we may unload the passengers from this damned ship.'

'In this weather?' Bradford objected. 'It is almost the depth of winter, and the snow flurries become more numerous every day. Even on the shoreline there is snow underfoot.'

'How long do you think we shall need to construct the necessary houses?' Winslow asked.

'Of that I cannot be certain,' said Standish, 'but I would suggest that we place a man in charge of that as his only labour. We shall need to fell trees and convert them into huts, however crude, that will keep out the elements.'

'I know the very man,' Bradford smiled. 'Thomas Bailey's father was a carpenter and woodsman, and while we were living in Gainsborough, in very poor conditions, Thomas hewed timber and repaired such buildings as we had.'

'I had rather hoped to recruit him in the defence of our township against native tribes,' Standish objected.

Brewster shook his head. 'What is there to defend, if there be no houses? It was you who pointed out that our first priority must be to release the community from the holds of this pestilential vessel. You may make a soldier of him later, but first he must build houses. We should allocate several other able-bodied men to his supervision.'

'We must also hunt for food and plant crops,' John Carver reminded them. 'I have some experience of maintaining a vegetable garden, so I will undertake to dig the first plot and plant the first seed, although that must await the warmer weather. In the meantime, we seemed destined to live on fish, unless there be game to be had in the woods.'

One by one the priorities were identified. Each day the shallop was launched over the side of the *Mayflower* in order to take a small party led by Standish, with his musket at the ready, across the bay to the shoreline. They occasionally came across the remnants of native huts with mats still inside, and from time to time they dug hopefully under mounds of earth, most of which proved to be native graves. They hastily refilled these with as much ceremony as time permitted, William Brewster intoning a blessing over each one. Some mounds yielded corn and other food that had obviously been stored against the winter, and the foraging party argued over whether they should pilfer their contents. They ultimately decided that they would, but resolved that should the natives return to retrieve their possessions, the colony would reward them with gold coin.

Each expedition also returned with fresh fish, which Mary Brewster, Rose Standish and Elizabeth Winslow found new ways of cooking in the hope of encouraging those below decks to eat it. They were accompanied at all times by Joanna Tasker, who was usually referred to as Joanna Bailey in acknowledgement of her adopted father. Joanna was being taught to cook, but also tended the sick. She felt responsible for not having done more to save her mother, and she sought to ease her guilt by looking after the suffering passengers.

It was only two weeks short of Christmas Day when the advance party led by Standish stepped onto the final beach that they had seen from a distance on board the *Mayflower*. It resembled all the others they had landed on, except that it had a heavily wooded hill behind it that promised much timber for housebuilding, while the immediate foreshore appeared to have been cleared for settlement, presumably by previous native tribes. The suspicion that they were taking over a former native village was confirmed when they came across more grave mounds that were partly overgrown, and former food pits that now contained only shrivelled mush. But another pit contained corn seed that had been stored for future planting, and the advance party carried it back to the *Mayflower* with the happy news that Plymouth had finally been located.

There was no time to lose in building accommodation on shore, if only to prevent the further spread of the disease that had broken out below decks. It was typified by a hacking cough and breathlessness. Plymouth foreshore was soon populated with graves, each with a wooden cross on which had been carved the name of the person lying beneath it.

Spurred on by the need to provide better shelter from the snowfall that marked the first month of 1621, those delegated the task set about creating huts along the shoreline, but above the obvious mark of high tide. Thomas stepped ashore for the first time, armed with several axes, a doubled-handed wood saw, a set of hammers, a pick and a shovel. He had been given three other men to assist him, and he instructed two of them to dig an oblong trench twenty feet square and five feet deep that would serve as the foundations of the first intended building, a common house for worship. As he did so, Standish called out to him and walked over, carrying a musket and several other items.

'Time for your first lesson, Master Bailey, before you venture into those woods.'

'I need no lessons in felling trees,' Thomas replied coolly.

Standish nodded. 'Indeed, I believe that you do not. But who knows what you might encounter in that forest behind us? The enemy may be hiding in the undergrowth, and you must be able to defend yourself.'

'We have no enemy of whom I am aware,' Thomas said, bridling, 'but we soon will have if we begin shooting at natives without enquiring as to their business.'

'You speak their language?' Standish asked sarcastically. 'And if not, do they speak English, think you? There will be only one common tongue between us and the enemy, and it will be the voice of musket fire. These natives will not have encountered artillery before and will run at the first volley.'

'I will not kill a man simply because I cannot parley with him,' Thomas insisted.

Standish changed tack. 'Even if that be the case, will you simply stand and let a wild beast rip you apart, when I can teach you to defend yourself? You may conduct matters as you will once you go into those trees, but I will not let you do so until you have learned the art of flintlock musketry.'

For the next half hour, Standish taught Thomas the necessary actions of loading a musket ball, ramming it home down the barrel of the weapon, adding powder to the pan and pulling back the hammer, ready for firing. He was advised to keep the weapon pre-loaded at all times, so that if called upon he need only bring the long barrel into the firing position and pull the hammer. Once satisfied that the action had become second nature to Thomas, he wished him Godspeed and allowed him to lead his two assistants into the pine woods that lay behind the beach in order to begin the felling process.

Late on the second day, they had felled several tall pines and split them down their grain using wooden pegs. They then cut them to a standard fifteen-foot length and manhandled them down to the area designated for housing, where two other men had dug the necessary oblong foundations into which the logs were dropped, then rammed down hard before the soil was replaced and trodden down in order to ensure that the logs remained upright. After a further two days they had enough to complete the walls, and the men who had dug the trenches were assigned the task of collecting bark from the nearest trees and weaving it into the slight gaps between the upright logs, in order to provide a full seal against the elements once daubed with mud. Then Thomas set off again to fell more trees that could be split and cut into suitable lengths to shape the roof.

He was halfway through felling a giant cedar when he stopped for a short break and a drink of water from the small stream that ran through the area. His musket was propped up against a nearby tree, fully loaded and primed as usual, when he caught sight of a furtive movement in a cluster of bushes a few yards further up the slope. Believing it to be a deer, or some other small animal that might be added to the pot that was kept constantly boiling below decks on the *Mayflower*, he reached across for his gun, never taking his eyes off the bushes. He checked the position of the hammer and took careful aim at the centre of the foliage; then some instinct made him lower the weapon just as a figure rose uncertainly from behind it.

She was the first native Thomas had ever beheld, not much older than Joanna. She was dressed in animal hides, and she slowly spread out her arms to indicate that she was carrying no weapon. Not knowing how to address a native, Thomas lowered the weapon completely and smiled. The girl smiled back, then indicated with her arm that she intended to move away. Unable to think of any other response, Thomas raised his arm in a friendly waving gesture, and called out, 'Go in peace.' The girl turned and scampered back up the slope as Thomas gave a silent thanks to God for staying his impulse to shoot.

Back on the shoreline he instructed two of the men who were digging more foundation trenches to accompany him into the forest to begin splitting the large trunk that he had felled. He opted to say nothing, particularly to Standish, regarding his encounter with the native girl. For one thing, he had no wish to encourage the eager military man to demonstrate his prowess as a soldier by hunting down an innocent girl. Furthermore, he did not want the men to be diverted from hut construction in order to go investigating.

The sickness on the *Mayflower* had now killed almost half of those who had set sail from Plymouth several months ago. Most of those who succumbed were women, including Rose Standish and Elizabeth Winslow. Only Susanna White, wife of Selector William White, Katherine Carver, Eleanor Billington, Elizabeth Hopkins and Mary Brewster were left alive, as well as Joanna, who was now installed in a hut alongside Thomas and had undertaken cooking duties for the men on shore. The future looked bleak for the birth of further children to swell the colony, although Susanna White had given birth below decks in November.

In order to avoid the contagion as much as possible, people had begun to venture onshore to occupy the huts that Thomas and his team of labourers had thrown up. Each hut was no more than ten feet square, had an earth floor, and was almost devoid of any furniture, but it was a welcome release from the ship's stinking hold. The first hut to be constructed was already in constant use, both as a chapel for religious services and as a place for Governor Carver and his selectors to discuss priorities.

The worst of that winter seemed to have receded, and a pale March sun was warming the shoulders of the group of men who sat outside the chapel. They were discussing where the next huts were to be located and counting in their heads how many able-bodied men they had available to help construct them, when Standish leapt to his feet and pointed at something. The others looked round, and it fell deathly quiet.

A native man stood in the centre of the new settlement of Plymouth, stern-faced but unarmed apart from a spear embedded in the ground in front of him. His torso was wrapped in animal skins, and on the top of his shaven head was a simple band of woven reed containing a single red feather.

As Standish walked swiftly towards him, Thomas called out, 'Offer him no harm, in case he comes in peace!'

To their astonishment, the man smiled and replied in their own tongue. 'Yes, peace. But this is our land, and you steal our corn.'

13

It fell silent until the man spoke again.

'This was my home until sickness came. It is called "Pawtucket". I leave with Smith and Hunt as guide to them, and I learn your language.'

'This was your home?' Brewster echoed.

The man nodded. 'I was child here. Then I go trading many times with white men. When I come back, I find many dead from great sickness, and I go live with Chief Massasoit of the Pokanoket people, who are Wampanoag.'

'You come from the local tribe?' Bradford asked.

'I am named "Samoset", and I watch as your big vessel come here and dig up the graves of those before me. But you do not take bones — only corn seed.'

'We were careful not to desecrate your graves,' Brewster assured him, 'and we said prayers to our God for their peaceful rest in Heaven.'

'You have the same god as the English warrior chief?' Samoset asked. 'He is a powerful god and brings much goodness to followers.'

'We are here because we wish to worship that God,' Brewster added eagerly. 'The English king — the "warrior chief" — now punishes those who seek to worship God as He should be worshipped, so we came here.'

'You bring the power of your god?' Samoset asked, clearly impressed. 'I also wish for the power of your god, so I told Massasoit of him. When I tell Massasoit I saw your big ship, he send me here to parley. He wishes for peace with you.'

'And we with you,' Standish assured him as he laid his musket on the ground. 'We mean no harm to your people.'

Samoset nodded towards Thomas. 'This man show peace to a girl named "Sokanon" — in your language, "Much Rain" — who come with me to look on your workings here. He does not kill her, so he is man of peace.'

'What is he referring to?' Standish asked as he turned to Thomas.

Thomas reddened slightly. 'I didn't tell you at the time, but a few days ago there was a native girl spying on me in the trees back there while I was cutting more timbers. She ran away.'

'Did you shoot at her?'

'No — I just smiled and told her to go in peace. What reason did I have for shooting at her? She showed no sign of aggression towards me.'

'But you failed to report that there were natives in the trees?'

'I saw only her,' Thomas replied.

Brewster called them both back to the business in hand. 'It seems to me that thanks to Thomas's forbearance we may have a useful connection with the local natives, who can ensure that we continue to live in peace with them.'

'We seek peace,' Samoset reasserted, 'and you seek corn seed.'

'We had intended to pay you for it,' Brewster explained, 'but we need it for our next crop, since the seed we planted some weeks ago seems not to have taken.'

'This land not good for growing,' Samoset explained. 'Where Massasoit has a dwelling is better for growing.'

Bradford invited Samoset to take a seat on the ground with them and sent Thomas to collect beer from the communal store.

After his second mug, Samoset proved more than content to tell his life story, and then — at Standish's urging — to explain where the native tribes closest to Plymouth Colony were located. He had grown up where the colony now was, which had then been a native village called Pawtucket. His first encounter with white settlers had occurred when an English expedition led by John Smith and Thomas Hunt ventured across to Newfoundland in search of fish, then explored the woods to the south, along the coastline that they had named Cape Cod Bay, for furs that they might take back to England. It was at this time that Samoset was hired by them as a guide to the forests and fishing banks, and learned his rudimentary English.

John Smith had then sailed back to England in one of the fleet's vessels, and a different side of Thomas Hunt emerged when he captured a group of natives and took them back as slaves to English households. Several of them, including a friend of Samoset's named Squanto, had escaped and persuaded another English merchant called Thomas Dermer to bring him back across the Atlantic, where they slipped ashore once they were back home. Squanto walked for many months until he encountered the Wampanoag settlement of Sowams, a few hours north of Plymouth on the upper waters of Cape Code Bay. There he met up again with Samoset and learned that their home village of Pawtucket had been abandoned after a fever had decimated its inhabitants. He had therefore gone to live under the protection of Massasoit, the sachem chief of the Pokanoket tribe, part of the Wampanoag confederacy of families living in various tribal villages to the north of Plymouth.

Samoset promised to return in a few days with his friend Squanto, whose grasp of English was better than his. Brewster gave him a cross he had sculpted from local wood and asked him to show it to his chief, as a sign that the settlers in the former native village were men of God who could be trusted.

A week later, everyone in the colony's hutted area stopped what they were doing and stared with a mixture of amazement and fear as a group of twenty or so natives emerged silently from the trees and walked into the open space in the centre of the settlement. Standish hurried over to where Thomas was showing two labourers how to properly seal the latest hut they had constructed, and whispered hoarsely, 'Place a loaded musket just inside the door of that hut next to you. Be prepared to employ it to good effect.'

Thomas glared at him. 'I will choose when — and if — to loose my weapon at what may prove to be friendly natives. For the moment, let us see what they want.'

The two men joined Brewster, Bradford, Carver and Winslow and waited until the native group halted on a murmured instruction from the man in the centre, whose ornate headdress marked him out from the rest. He then gave a curt order, and twenty spears were rammed into the ground in unison. A man stepped forward and addressed the settlers.

'I am Squanto, and I come in peace with my brothers. We bring our sachem — you say "chief" — whose name is Massasoit.' He called out in his native tongue to the man in the ornate headdress, who stepped forward and bowed. Samoset said something to him, and he moved closer to Brewster. Standish made to move between the two men, before Brewster waved him back.

'Stand further off, Myles, since we must take them at their word and show them friendship.'

Standish did as instructed. Squanto smiled and said something to Chief Massasoit, who walked to within a few feet of Brewster and stooped in order to place a pile of furs on the ground in front of him.

'A gift of peace,' Squanto announced.

Brewster removed a wooden cross from around his neck. He stepped forward and placed it on the pile of furs. 'Our God blesses your gift. We have food and drink for you, in a gesture of our wish to be your friends.'

Squanto translated, and everyone on both sides seemed to be relieved that this first exchange had gone well. A few minutes later, they were sharing beer and corn bread in a wide circle on the dusty ground. Squanto demonstrated his grasp of English as he acted as interpreter for Chief Massasoit, who began to explain the recent history of the native tribes by which the colonists were surrounded. Standish made a careful mental note of what they were being told, and instructed Thomas to do likewise.

It emerged that the tribes to their north were united in a loose coalition known as the Wampanoag people, which subsumed many smaller tribes, including those from which both Samoset and Squanto came. They had formed this coalition in order to defend themselves against another coalition of native tribes to the south known collectively as Narragansetts, who were fierce warriors dedicated to preserving their fishing and hunting grounds from all other tribes.

The Plymouth Colony leaders were left in no doubt that the Narragansetts would regard the recent invasion of white settlers as a challenge to their traditional lifestyle, and would attack without parleying first. Massasoit followed up this gloomy prediction with an offer to combine his native tribes with the colonists, an arrangement that would offer protection to both groups.

Standish sneered and muttered to Governor Carver. 'They are clearly the weaker of two warring tribes, and they seek our superior arms. Why should we side with either tribe? Better to rely on our own resources for our defence, rather than provoke a group of natives who, according to this man here, are the strongest in the region.'

'We come here in friendship, to offer you protection and instruction on how to grow your food,' Squanto replied angrily. 'We offer to teach you how to hunt and fish. Do you reject our friendship?'

'Keep silent, Myles,' Governor Carver ordered him, as he turned back to address Squanto. 'Our apologies for the fact that our man here has the manners of a soldier. But he raises a concern that I share. If we join with you, will we not anger the Narragansetts?'

'You anger them already, simply by landing on this shore,' Squanto told him with a frown. 'They have bitter memories of other white faces who came some years ago and drove off their finest warriors as slaves, never to return home. They will give you no warning of any attack, nor will they come to you in friendship, as we have done. But even if you reject our offer to protect you should the Narragansetts attack, do you not need our help to plant crops, hunt beasts, and fish in the waters?'

'He certainly has a valid point there,' Brewster conceded, 'so let us leave the matter of warfare for another time.' He raised his head so that he was speaking directly to Chief Massasoit, even though he would not understand what Brewster was saying. 'We accept your friendship as loving followers of our God, and we would wish to learn your ways in the matters of growing food, hunting the beasts of the forest, and reaping the harvests of the waters. Be assured that should you be attacked by other tribes, our weapons will help to defend you, since our God does not permit the taking of human life.'

Squanto duly translated, and the chief smiled. He engaged in a lengthy conversation with Squanto in their native tongue, and several of the men who accompanied him stepped forward. Squanto turned back to speak to the colonist group again. 'These brothers will show you their skills. Who are those among you who lead the hunting parties?'

Standish claimed that right and was led off into the forest by a native man armed with a spear. Then it was the turn of Governor Carver himself, who had a vegetable plot beside his hut that had been planted with some of the stolen corn seed, but had thus far seen no shoots from the ground, even though it was now well into spring. Another native man walked down to the shoreline and returned with some dried seaweed, which he laid into a new trench. He then reached into a sack at his side and dropped new seed on top of it, before covering up the trench and muttering a few words in his native tongue.

Finally, two of the colonists designated by Carver were sent down to the shore with another native teacher, where they were shown how to trap shellfish and net other fish. They brought their trophies back up with them, and for the next two nights the Plymouth congregation hosted and toasted their native neighbours with lobster, oysters and roast venison. On the third day the group led by Massasoit took its leave with many bows, handshakes and translated promises of lasting friendship.

Brewster's mind was clouded by thoughts of possible conflict that might arise if the male colonists, most of whom were without wives, were to show any sexual interest in the native women. His next sermon was therefore based upon the virtue of celibacy, the evils of fleshly desires, and the purity of Christian practices. As he spoke, Thomas thought of Joanna, who was rapidly approaching womanhood. One day she would need to seek a husband, and he dwelt uneasily on the prospect of contests between the men for her hand in marriage, and even possible bloodshed as a result. He raised his concerns with Brewster following the service, and the wise old man nodded and called over to Governor Carver.

'John, Master Bailey here has raised a matter over which we require your authority as governor.'

'Speak freely, William,' Carver replied invitingly, and the three men drew to one side.

'When is the *Mayflower* due to set sail on its homeward journey?' asked Brewster.

'Any day now,' Carver told him. 'The crew is greatly reduced, due to the sickness that took so many of our number, but Captain Jones assures me that with this prevailing westerly he should be able to steer her back to London with what men he has left. Why?'

'We — by which I mean you, of course — must arm him with a letter advising him of the need for more supplies, most particularly of seed for future crops. We are blessed that the natives have shown us so much regarding how to survive, but without new seed, we cannot hope to do so healthily. We have some beaver furs that we may send back, as a sign of the wealth that is to be found in these parts, but we must impress upon them that our first winter bore harshly upon us, and that we are greatly reduced in number. If their investment is to bear profit, we need more settlers, most particularly those with skills in farming and hunting. But above all we need women of child-bearing age who can boost our numbers. We have had but two new births since our arrival here, and there is only Joanna Bailey who is available for marriage. If single women might be encouraged to voyage out to join us, this would ensure the growth of the colony.'

'I shall write as you suggest,' Carver agreed. 'However, there is another matter that your words have recalled to my mind.' He hesitated, and his face reddened. 'It concerns Mistress Bailey. There have been mutterings among the congregation, and I have begun to receive representations in my capacity as Governor...'

'To what do you allude?' Thomas asked angrily. 'Joanna has been guilty of no offence of which I am aware. On the contrary, she has proved to be of great service in the tending of the sick. I fail to see...'

Carver raised his hand to silence him, then continued. 'It is not that, Thomas. Indeed, I hear nothing but praise for her Christian work here among us.'

'Then what?' Thomas demanded.

Carver took a deep breath. 'It is the matter of where she resides, Thomas.'

'She resides with me — her father. Would you rather that she resided somewhere where she might fall into evil ways?'

'But you are not her father, are you?' Carver reminded him. 'Not her father by blood, that is. And while you are to be commended for having taken her in out of the goodness of your heart when her mother died...'

'I took her in out of the natural love of a father for his daughter!' Thomas protested as his temper rose.

Carver stepped backwards. 'But to others within our congregation, less given to such charity, and less minded to attribute such worthy motives to you, might it not seem … well…?'

Thomas quivered with indignation. 'Say it! Spell out what evil thought besmirches your filthy, ungodly, sinful, cesspit of a mind!'

'Not me, Thomas — others,' Carver persisted.

'Including me,' Brewster added.

Thomas looked with incredulity from one to the other. 'You think that I might entertain carnal thoughts towards a child such as Joanna?'

'She is barely a child now, Thomas,' said Brewster. 'She is almost of an age when a man might think of seeking her hand in marriage. She is also at risk of being foully mistreated and betrayed.'

'And you think me capable of that, say you?' Thomas spat. Both men shook their heads, but Thomas was not appeased. He turned on Brewster. 'Did you not just accuse me of the same?'

'I merely meant that the circumstances were such as might give rise to such unworthy thoughts.'

'Only in the heads of those who have such lewd inclinations.'

'Of whom we unhappily have a few,' said Brewster. 'We say merely that to avoid such unworthy speculation…'

'I must move out of my own hut, built with my own hands — is that what you are saying?'

'Regrettably, that is what we are recommending,' Brewster confirmed, and he and Carver hurriedly took their leave.

Thomas returned to his hut and reluctantly put the proposal to Joanna. She shook her head at the mere thought that her father would abandon her to live alone, then demanded to know why. Thomas shrank from referring to the evil thoughts of others, and simply suggested that the hut would become a little overcrowded as Joanna came into her adulthood. She made a tutting noise and reminded him that she was not yet fourteen years of age. 'So what is the real reason, Father? Do you no longer love me? Do I smell too badly for you to share a hut with me? What has led to this disturbing suggestion?'

Thomas could think of nothing to say that would make any sense to the girl, so he let the matter drop and went back out for a walk. In the distance he saw the tall masts of the *Mayflower* bobbing up and down, and he reflected on happier times when he could enjoy being 'Dadda' without malicious tongues wagging. He cursed Governor Carver and those with such wicked, carnal, imaginations.

Two days later, Thomas regretted his uncharitable thoughts about John Carver when he received the news that he was dead.

Always a keen horticulturalist, Carver had been digging his garden plot under a hot April sun when he complained of a sharp pain in his head. The pain persisted even when he lay down in the shade of his hut; then he lapsed into a fevered delirium that ended with his death. Six weeks later, his distraught widow Katherine died of a broken heart, and they were both buried with considerable ceremony in the common burial ground that now contained over sixty simple crosses. It was put to Thomas that he was now free to occupy the former Carver hut, and he reluctantly advised a tearful Joanna that he had been ordered to move by the new Governor of Plymouth, his long-time friend William Bradford, elected by unanimous acclaim.

It was of little consolation to Thomas that the same congregation that elected Bradford also agreed that Master Bailey should be elected as a selector to fill the vacancy created by Bradford's elevation. Thomas was now a senior member of the community with his own living accommodation, but he would have preferred to be back in Leiden with Amy and their daughter.

14

Prior to his death John Carver had been assiduous in tending his garden, following the processes revealed to him by Squanto and his fellow tribesmen regarding the best way to grow corn. Thomas was now expected to take over responsibility for that garden, in accordance with the ordinance issued by Carver and his former selectors that every family allocated ground for the construction of a hut must also grow crops alongside it. These would then be consigned to the communal food store.

As Thomas looked with satisfaction at the green corn stalks standing proudly in rows, he worried about Joanna, left by herself. Her tear-streaked face had clearly reflected her feelings of abandonment, and he had come close to revealing that his only reason for vacating their hut was in order to preserve her reputation. But he had held his tongue as Joanna had flung her arms around him and pleaded, 'Come back, Dadda, when I prove to you that I am worthy.'

They met up regularly in the bustling activity of the community. Standing beside the grave of Katherine Carver, they were reminded of their own grief.

'A pity that Mamma died at sea,' Joanna mumbled as she clung to Thomas's arm. 'If she had died here, we would have a grave marker of our own that we could visit every Sunday, as the others do.'

Thomas looked down at her sad face. 'We do not need her body buried in the earth in order to remember her in the same way. We need only seek the permission of the selectors to plant a memorial cross of our own, and we can come here like all the others to pay our respects to her memory.'

The selectors approved their request. Each Sunday, after the morning service, Thomas and Joanna would link hands as they stood looking down at the ornate wooden cross that Thomas had made, and he would say a prayer of his own devising, hoping that God would not be offended by his amateur efforts. Those weekly visits kept them together, as he laboured in tree felling and crop tending, and she continued to learn wifely skills from the ageing Mary Brewster. Joanna also enjoyed the friendship of Mary's daughter Patience, who was now a grown woman and was promised to Samuel Fuller.

Joanna was showing promise as a children's nurse and nanny, and regularly supervised the daily exercise of three-year-old Damaris Hopkins, daughter of Selector Stephen Hopkins and his wife Elizabeth. The only girl of Joanna's approximate age was Fear Brewster, the fifteen-year-old second daughter of William and Mary Brewster, but she was somewhat sickly, and rarely wandered beyond the confines of their family hut.

As he tended his garden, Thomas's reverie was disturbed by the voice of Governor William Bradford.

'You seem to have a way with those plants, Thomas. Mine are a few weeks behind yours, but God willing we should have a fine crop come Harvest Festival.'

'Have we suddenly gone all Anglican?' Thomas teased. 'Isn't "Harvest Festival" one of their observances?'

'It is indeed, but it is well meant. It gives thanks to God for the bounty of His earth, and we should consider doing something similar.'

'We could call it the "Giving Thanks" observance,' Thomas suggested.

'A little clumsy,' Bradford replied. 'How about "Thanksgiving"?'

'That sounds appropriate, assuming that we have something for which to give thanks other than tables strewn with corn bowls.'

'Didn't the natives teach you how to bring down deer and other meats?' Bradford asked. 'And Edward Winslow has proved himself a fine purveyor of ocean harvests, since he supplied all the shellfish at his wedding breakfast when he married Widow White. We can bring a harvest of good victuals to the table when the corn is garnered, and I have half a mind to invite the natives who made it all possible by teaching us their skills.'

His proposal was eagerly adopted by the Assembly. As the days began to shorten, and the corn crop was lifted, an invitation was sent to Massasoit through the good offices of Squanto, who was an almost daily visitor to Plymouth Colony. The Plymouth men set about snaring wildfowl, shooting deer and trapping shellfish. The few women of the settlement set about cooking day and night, after digging holes in the ground to use as ovens, in the manner taught to them by the natives.

On the appointed day the natives arrived in large numbers with Massasoit at their head, flanked by Squanto and Samoset. As they came to a halt in front of the crude log tables constructed specially for the occasion under Thomas's supervision, several young natives stepped forward bearing deer carcasses that were instantly seized upon by the settler women and put into pits full of slow-burning wood. These, combined with the venison that had already been cooked, along with shellfish, wild turkey and platters of assorted fruits such as plums and grapes, kept the combined assembly feasting and celebrating for several days.

At the beginning of the festivities, Brewster led them all in the singing of Psalm 100, with its emphasis on entering the

Kingdom of Heaven as a united people singing God's praises. The natives responded with a few dances of their own intended to appease the gods of the weather, and ensure healthy crops for the white men amongst them. On this occasion there were also native women, and Standish cast disparaging glances at the lingering looks that some of the male settlers were giving them.

'How long before fighting breaks out, when our men seek out their women?' he asked Thomas sourly.

'Surely our religion teaches men to suppress their lusts?' Thomas replied, embarrassed.

'Does it?' Standish asked cynically. 'Whatever the cause, there will be warfare between our two nations before long, mark my words. And Squanto advises me that the Narragansett tribes have begun to gather on an island to the south of here; he fears that they are amassing war parties, and that we should be preparing to defend ourselves.'

'In what way?' Thomas asked. 'Until we receive fresh supplies, we have but a half dozen muskets, and would be ill placed to withstand a concerted attack. Perhaps we should, after all, accept the offer of protection by alliance that Squanto gave on his first visit here.'

'And thereby hoist our colours firmly to the mast? Do you think that Massasoit and his followers are here at our feast simply because they appreciate our cooking and have acquired a taste for our nettle beer? They are here because they wish us to join with them against the Narragansetts, and for all we know the Narragansetts would be prepared to make a similar alliance with us against the Wampanoag. Neither of them appreciates how ill provisioned we are in the matter of fire power, but see us as powerful allies.'

'Perhaps we should keep it that way,' Thomas suggested, 'at least until we get more supplies. Do we know when that is likely to be?'

'Anyone's guess,' Standish muttered. 'Given the delays we experienced, battling our way over here against an unfavourable wind, supplies could be months away. Even then, we have no idea if those in London will respond to our request, given that we sent them no substantial token of wealth to be obtained from the land we have settled. They care not about any desire on the part of Governor Bradford and Pastor Brewster to establish a Kingdom of God in this forsaken spot — they care only for riches, and a healthy return on their investment.'

'Say you think they could abandon us out here?' Thomas asked disbelievingly. 'Surely it's their Christian duty to those they sent out here to ensure that we do not wither and die?'

'It is also their duty to those who invested their wealth in their enterprise to ensure that there is profit to be made from us. That's all we are to them.'

'So what are we to do in the way of defence?'

'*You* must fell more trees, and I must organise men to construct a palisade from them. We need a strong barrier of tree trunks, ten feet high at least, with a platform a few feet below the parapet, from which we can fend off any attack from natives.'

'Yet we have only a handful of muskets,' Thomas reminded him. 'They take time to reload and can — even if fired with accuracy — kill only one man at a time.'

'Indeed, you have the nub of it,' Standish nodded. 'There are two possible remedies for that disadvantage. The first is that the natives will never have encountered musket fire, and they will scatter at the first volley. The second is that you can

141

construct bows and arrows just like theirs and teach the men how to use them in the manner of our ancestors at Crecy and Agincourt.'

'The more we speak, the more convinced I am that we should parley with the tribes to the south,' Thomas mused.

Standish shook his head. 'Thereby provoking the tribes to our north?'

'So what say you?'

'I say that you begin felling more timber without delay, to build this palisade of which I spoke, while I train the men in its purpose. I shall also train up men to reload muskets that others may fire. Pray God that the powder and shot hold out against any attack, and that fresh supplies arrive before the Narragansetts advance upon us.'

Work commenced as required, and from dawn to dusk the hutted area overlooking the foreshore echoed with the thud of the axes wielded by Thomas and his crew of woodsmen. The branches they cut were used as firewood, while the trunks were lowered into a trench facing back towards the rapidly diminishing forest through which it was anticipated that the Narragansetts would attack. Once the main forward palisade was in place, and a platform installed five feet from its top, trenches were dug down either side, until the settlement was protected on three sides. This left only the approach from the bay itself, which Standish believed could be defended without the need for a palisade.

The first of the winter snow had begun to fall when shouts of delight went up from somewhere inside the three-sided compound. Settlers began pointing at the three square sails in the distance as a triple-masted merchant vessel made its way steadily towards the Plymouth shoreline. A welcome party raced down to the water's edge to cheer as the *Fortune* dropped anchor, and to welcome ashore the captain, Thomas Barton, who was led with great rejoicing to meet with Governor Bradford in the Meeting Room. The usual greetings were exchanged, and Bradford asked eagerly, 'What supplies do you bring us?'

Barton looked uneasy. His gaze dropped to the earth floor, and he replied, 'My cargo is human only. I bring you thirty-five more recruits for your settlement; thirty-three of them are men, who will be a great asset in your endeavours to found a colony here.'

'Only two women?' Bradford yelled in disbelief.

Barton nodded. 'It was thought that you would most benefit from labouring hands. Of the two women, one is now a widow, her husband having died during the voyage. She is, as we speak, in the throes of childbirth, and she already has a son who has voyaged with her.'

'Who is attending her in her labour?' Mary Brewster asked.

Barton shrugged. 'The only other woman on board is Elizabeth Bassett, and her own husband is sick, so she is more occupied in tending to him.'

'This will not do!' Mary exclaimed. 'We need every child we can bring into this society of ours, so I must go on board and see to her needs. I shall take others with me, including Joanna Bailey, if that meets with your approval, Thomas?'

Thomas nodded. 'Did you not bring us more arms, along with powder and shot?' he asked.

Barton shook his head. 'Nought was said to me of the need to load a cargo other than the settlers.'

'So you bring us some thirty more mouths to feed, and nothing to feed them *with*?' Brewster demanded with uncharacteristic petulance. 'What said your charterers regarding the need to keep us supplied?'

'Nought, to me at least,' Barton replied as he reached inside his leather surcoat, 'but they bid me hand this letter to your governor.'

Bradford took the letter, tore off the seal and began reading. His face became flushed with anger, and he finally threw the missive onto the ground as he looked around at the Council members to either side of him. 'It would seem that our sponsors in London were not impressed with the few furs that we were able to send them, nor with the fact that the *Mayflower* had rocks for ballast when she set sail from here. They say that there will be no more supplies unless we fill the hold of this new vessel with riches to demonstrate that we are capable of rewarding their investment. In short, we would appear to be abandoned to our fate.'

There was a stunned silence, broken by a polite cough from Barton.

'I need to disembark my passengers without delay and fill my hold with whatever bounty you can supply. Have you shelter for those who come ashore?'

With extremely bad grace, Governor Bradford began identifying those huts in which there was space for others. Thomas found himself playing host to a carpenter called John Adams and a labourer called Edward Bompasse, both of whom he quickly put to work making crude furniture such as bed bolsters, tables and chairs. As a result of the influx of new mouths to feed, the already meagre winter rations of the settlement were halved. For the next few weeks, the general atmosphere among the huts was one of sullen resentment — except in the hut that had formally belonged to Thomas.

Joanna came scampering excitedly into the open area at the side of Thomas's hut as he was admiring the dovetail joints that John Adams was employing to close the ends of a bed to its sides. She was accompanied by a tall, willowy youth and was carrying a bundle, which she lowered for him to admire.

'See, Dadda! A baby girl! Her name is Martha Ford, like her mother — and this is John, Martha's other child! He's two years older than me — isn't he handsome?'

Thomas experienced a pang of alarm. He looked the gangly boy up and down and asked, 'How strong are you?'

'Strong enough,' John replied.

Thomas grinned. 'Good! They need willing hands down at the water's edge, filling the empty barrels of the *Fortune* with beaver furs to ship back to England. Your people may have come out here without supplies, but hopefully those who sent you will have a change of heart when they see that we can produce something of value to them.'

'John just came to say "Hello",' Joanna protested.

'He didn't need to,' Thomas replied, 'since you did it for him. Right now, I want him down at the water's edge.'

'You don't like him, do you?' Joanna pouted as she watched John walking towards the workers on the shoreline.

Thomas shrugged. 'I don't know him yet, do I? Who exactly is he, and where is he from?'

'His name is John Ford, and he and his mother have been sent to live in our hut. His mother gave birth to this sweet baby girl called Martha just as the ship was arriving here, and I helped Mistress Brewster to deliver her. I'm looking after her for the moment, while her mother is visiting Mistress Brewster to enquire if anyone needs any sewing to be done.'

'So you've become a baby nurse, have you?' Thomas smiled kindly. 'Not to mention a friend to young Master Ford?'

Joanna blushed. 'He doesn't have very much to say for himself, but he's very sweet and attentive.'

'Not *too* attentive, I hope,' said Thomas as the smile left his face. 'But hopefully we can put him to good use.'

'It would seem that you already have,' came a stern voice from behind them, and Thomas looked round to see a woman with jet black hair, an oval face and deep blue eyes.

Joanna made the introductions. 'Dadda, this is Martha Ford. Martha, this is my father.'

'Presumably the one who sent my son down to the water's edge without first consulting me?' Martha demanded.

Thomas stiffened. 'I was unaware that I required your permission, since I took your son — if he be the young man called John who was here momentarily — to be an adult. That being the case, as a selector I'm entitled to set him to work on whatever seems to fit his talents. Or does he not possess any?'

'I don't care who — or what — you are, but my son John is not to be ordered around like some lowly servant. His father was well placed where we lived in Rochester and was the most popular brewer in the town. John was apprenticed to him.'

'Some reversal of fortune must have led you to come out here to this far-flung corner of God's Earth, where it does not matter *who* — or *what* — you once were,' Thomas told her coldly. 'All that matters out here is what you are now, and how much you can contribute to the community.'

'I'm not sure I care for your manner,' Martha sniffed disapprovingly, 'but fortunately your lovely daughter here is possessed of an altogether more pleasing disposition. Presumably she acquired that from her mother, whom I am advised died during your voyage out here, as did my husband. It is perhaps the true measure of you that you apparently never married her mother, despite getting her with child.'

Joanna opened her mouth, intent on correcting the misapprehension, but Thomas beat her to it.

'Heaven forfend that I should possess a mind so intent on thinking ill of others, but you should be properly advised that Joanna is not my daughter by blood. Nor was her mother ever my wife or my mistress. But while we are speaking of such things, you should be advised that I do not approve of my thirteen-year-old daughter occupying the same hut as your fifteen-year-old son.'

'You wish him to sleep out in the open?'

'No, I wish him to move into this hut, which I share with two others. He can be apprenticed to me, should you wish him to learn a useful trade. He will learn how to hack down trees, build huts and defence palisades, hunt wildlife and catch fish. None of those occupations will, I feel sure, satisfy the high expectations that you and your late husband had for him, but they will ensure that he earns his keep. Now, good day to you.' He bowed sarcastically.

Martha Ford gave a snort of disapproval, turned on her heel and walked stiffly away.

'That was *very* rude, Father, and I shall expect you to apologise,' said Joanna. 'Martha Ford is a lovely lady, but clearly you are incapable of seeing a future for yourself in the married state!' She then hurried after Martha.

John Ford presented himself at Thomas's hut just before sunset, and Thomas handed over the bed that had been completed for his use only that day. The young lad seemed overawed in Thomas's company, but eagerly set about the tasks he was allocated. Within a month he was fulfilling a useful role in the colony. Thomas was wondering how best to approach his mother to tell her so, when there came a warning shout from the lookout on the platform behind the palisade.

Thomas raced into the hut for his pre-loaded musket and called to John to take cover. Then he walked briskly out into the open and raised his weapon as several native warriors rose to their full height between the trees and loaded their bows. Then Thomas stared in fascination as other native warriors set fire to the ends of the arrows, and the bowmen leaned back in order to gain maximum range for their missiles.

The first of the natives fell to a well-aimed musket ball from the palisade, and Thomas watched in horror as an arrow sailed a few feet over his head and landed on the thatch of his hut, which began blazing in the strong breeze. Thomas raced back into the hut, ordered John outside, and called for Adams and Bompasse to fetch pails of sea water to douse the flames.

He stepped back outside and began running towards the palisade carrying his musket. Halfway across the open space he caught sight of John Ford, frozen in terror as arrows began thunking into the ground all around him. Thomas threw down his musket and raced towards the youth, ordering him lie flat on the ground. John appeared not to comprehend, so Thomas attempted to push him down. Just as he did so, there was a whirring sound, followed by the dull thud of an arrow finding flesh. Thomas fell to the ground with a scream.

Another series of sharp sounds became audible above the clamour, and they soon became identifiable as war whoops from the shore. A line of canoes ground up the shingle, and from them leapt dozens of native warriors who answered to the command of Chief Massasoit. They raced up the outside of the palisade, waving axes, and the warriors who had attacked the Plymouth settlement took to their heels. It was over in less than thirty minutes, and the majority of the colonists continued extinguishing the flames that had threatened three huts, while a few of them checked for casualties.

It was John Ford who discovered Thomas lying on the ground with an arrow embedded in his shoulder.

15

When Thomas came round, the first thing he saw was the tear-streaked face of Joanna. He was lying on a bolster, and there was an intense burning pain in his left shoulder. He tried to wriggle, but Joanna gripped his hand in warning.

'Stay still, Dadda — it's almost finished.'

'What is?' he asked groggily.

'The repairs to your wound,' came the authoritative female voice from behind him. 'If you wriggle, I can't guarantee that the stitching will be straight, and with a scar this size you'd want it to look normal.'

'What are you stitching?'

'What do you think? The men got the arrow out of you, but it left a big hole. If it's not to become poisoned, it needs to be sealed up. Fortunately for you, I used to specialise in leatherwork, and I have the right sort of needles.'

'Who is that?' Thomas asked.

'My mother,' said John. 'Thank you for saving my life, by the way.'

'I didn't intend to,' Thomas replied modestly. 'You were stupidly remaining upright when I told you to lie flat on the ground, and I was about to push you down. Ouch!'

'That's what you get for being honest,' Martha told him sternly. 'If you want me to repeat that, just carry on telling me how little you cared for my son's life.'

'You misunderstand me,' Thomas protested. 'I *was* trying to save his life, in a sense. Remaining upright when there are arrows flying through the air is not only very stupid, but … ow!'

'That's for calling my son stupid,' Martha chuckled.

'You're enjoying this, aren't you?' Thomas complained.

'She's not, Dadda,' Joanna told him. 'When they first brought you back into your hut, she had tears in her eyes.'

'Silence, unless you want this needle in *your* rear end!' Martha threatened, and it fell quiet.

'How much longer?' Thomas demanded.

Martha sighed. 'Unless you want a fine depiction of Saint Peter and the Apostles in several coloured yarns, I'm almost finished. Then you can sit up.'

Several minutes later he did so, and Joanna handed him a mug of beer and a slice of cold venison after Martha had slipped outside, still complaining of Thomas's seeming ingratitude for her services.

'She had a very good point, Dadda — you never once said "thank you", and she really sewed your wound up very neatly.'

'I'll thank her in due course, when it stops hurting,' Thomas agreed reluctantly, 'but what happened after I was wounded? I take it that the natives were driven off?'

'Yes, there were some other natives who came from the bay and chased them through the trees. Some of them are still here, with Governor Bradford.'

'And trying to talk the old fool into some sort of peace treaty,' Standish added as he walked into the hut and smiled down at Thomas. 'You were very lucky, Thomas — an inch or two to the right and we wouldn't be having this conversation.'

'What was that about a peace treaty?' Thomas asked. 'We aren't at war with any of the natives, so far as I'm aware, so why would we need to sign a peace treaty?'

Standish sighed. 'It's perhaps as well that we value your services as a woodsman, because you make a poor military strategist. We were rescued from extinction by Massasoit. He is now trying to persuade Bradford that the attack on us by the Narragansetts was a declaration of war, and that we need the Pokanoket people that he leads, and the wider confederation of Wampanoag tribes, to protect us. He is even offering a native princess as a bride for one of our people, in order to seal that compact.'

'And what had Governor Bradford to say about that?' Thomas asked.

'He promised that he would put the proposal to the Council. You don't have a wife, so why don't you offer?'

'I'm far from being the only single man in the colony,' Thomas replied. 'If it comes to that, why don't you volunteer?'

Standish laughed lightly. 'A military leader like myself cannot afford to marry, and have a wife and family dependent upon him, when any day he may be taken from them in battle.'

Thomas remembered that Standish had been married and that his wife Rose had succumbed to that first harsh winter. He thought that perhaps Standish still mourned his wife, and he changed the subject. 'How did Massasoit and his warriors manage to drive off the Narragansetts? Did they succeed in scaling our palisade walls?'

'No,' Standish replied with a frown, 'they came from the water, and ran round the sides. Our first task must be to raise a palisade on the ocean side as well.'

'Thereby preventing any further assistance from Massasoit?'

'No, in order to prevent any further native incursion from the bay. You may not be able to fell trees for several months, but hopefully you have taught others how to do it, so once you're back on your feet you can presumably still supervise them?'

'I can fell trees!' John called out eagerly from a stool in the corner.

151

Thomas smiled back at him. 'Such eagerness, and the least you can do in return for my saving your life. We begin tomorrow morning.'

'What do you think of my mother now?' John asked Thomas the next day. He was taking a break from tree-felling, and he drank some water as he sat down on the ground.

Thomas was perched on a tree stump. He thought carefully before answering, fairly certain that whatever he said would be conveyed back to the lady in question. 'She is deft with a needle and thread, I'll say that for her. Those who have been able to view my wound say that the stitching has quite a professional appearance.'

John laughed, then looked more seriously at Thomas. 'I meant what do you think of her as a woman?'

Thomas shrugged. 'I am no judge of women, and I have barely spoken to her. Why do you ask?'

'I just wondered regarding her prospects of remarriage,' John replied sheepishly. 'I lost my father on the voyage, and you should at least be aware of how important a father is, even if you know nothing of women.'

'You miss having a father?'

'I miss my father, certainly. And so does Mamma. She cried for several days after he was cast into the sea, but then she had to attend to the birth of my little sister Martha. She'll have to grow up without a father, if Mamma doesn't remarry.'

'And you're seeking a husband for her, if I don't misjudge you?' Thomas asked.

John flushed. 'I just thought that perhaps, since you already have a daughter with no mother, and my mother has a daughter with no father…'

'Time to get back on your feet and cut down some more timber,' Thomas interrupted him brusquely. 'The light will be gone in a few hours, and Selector Standish grows impatient to see the final palisade wall constructed.'

The suggestion by Massasoit that the colonists declare an alliance with his combined Wampanoag tribes, sealed with a marriage treaty, was put to the congregation in a meeting. The congregation of Separatists had kept rigidly to their principles and beliefs since their days in Leiden, and had honoured the Compact they had signed on board the *Mayflower*. As a result, all important decisions were both debated and decided upon by a simple majority of those entitled to partake in the government of the colony, which meant all those who attended meetings and kept the Sabbath.

Standish eventually persuaded the congregation that to enter an alliance with any conglomeration of native tribes would be regarded as a sign of enmity by tribes that belonged to a different confederacy. Therefore, he argued the best position for the Plymouth folk to adopt was one of strict neutrality. They had few muskets with which to defend themselves until further supplies came from England, and it was possible that no more would be sent. There were other issues that underpinned the final decision. While not asserting that natives were any less God's children than their white neighbours, those who guided the colony in its religious observances were unsure whether it would be a sin in God's eyes for a white Christian man to marry a non-Christian native woman. Therefore, they were not certain whether they could accept Massasoit's offer of a native princess as a bride for one of the colonists.

Thomas did not regard himself as a military strategist, but the lingering pain in his shoulder reminded him daily that there would be no colony left had it not been for the Wampanoag. He could certainly corroborate Standish's assertion that they were insufficiently supplied with firearms to be able to resist any concerted attack, but it seemed to him that the remedy for that was an alliance with one powerful native tribe against another. This would, apart from anything else, eliminate one group of them as potential enemies.

One Sunday morning he stood outside his hut, wishing that he had married Amy so that he could have more tender memories of her, and he silently begged her forgiveness for his stubborn morality when she had run from a brutal marriage. Then he asked himself whether that thought was entirely his own, or whether it had been provoked by John's reference to his mother's lonely widowhood. There must be worse things than to lie in the warmth of a willing woman, he reminded himself, and it was not as if Martha Ford was not comely. Her hair was still the raven black that nature had intended, and her dark blue eyes reminded him of the ocean.

His eyes drifted up towards Burial Hill, and he realised with a start that Joanna was visiting her mother's cross without him. But she was not alone: not only was she standing alongside John Ford, but they were holding hands. He stepped out at a swift pace, and Joanna looked over her shoulder and spotted him on his way up the gentle mound. She said something to John, who kissed her quickly on the cheek and all but ran down the far side of the slope.

'That *was* John, was it not?' Thomas demanded.

Joanna nodded, slightly pink in the face.

'And you and he *were* holding hands?'

'I *am* fourteen, Dadda,' she replied defiantly.

He nodded. 'Indeed you are, and before too long you will no doubt become someone's wife as well as my daughter. Did you intend to consult me as to your choice?'

'What's wrong with John?'

'Nothing of which I'm aware, but my point is that I should be consulted before you approach the congregation leaders with a request that you be allowed to marry.'

'And what might *you* know about marriage?' Joanna goaded him. 'You never considered my mother to be worthy of your hand, and John tells me that you have no interest in Martha Ford either.'

Thomas sighed. 'When you are older, hopefully you will more fully understand these things, and live with the wisdom that comes from accepting God's commandments. When I first knew your mother, we were both too young for such fancies.'

'*How* young? Mother says that she was a mature woman when she first tried to tempt you into marriage.'

'She was merely in her teenage years, as was I. We were both in service, she as a kitchen hand and I as a gardener of sorts. Even so, we were both much older than you or John are at present.'

'So why did you not wed when you grew more mature in years?'

'You must understand that it was a time of great upheaval for our congregation. To escape persecution for our beliefs, we journeyed to the Low Countries. There I lost contact with her when we were obliged to work for different masters. When we finally met again, she was engaged to your father.'

'Is it true that he beat her, or did she abandon him for love of you?'

'The former. I was all for giving *him* a beating, but she dissuaded me. Then you came along and captured my heart in a different way.'

'But you still rejected my mother?'

'Only in a carnal sense. We remained very close as we watched you grow. She would be so proud to see you standing here today, revering her memory. She…' He choked on his tears, and she put a comforting hand on his arm.

'You truly loved her, didn't you?'

'Indeed I did, and these days I regret that I did not marry her when I had the opportunity.'

'But why did you not claim her once she left my father?'

'Because she was still a married woman, and if you understand the Scriptures, it would have been a sin. Your true father may still be alive, for all I know. While I might sin for myself, I could not ask her to perjure her immortal soul in that manner.'

'Well, Martha Ford is now a widow. Do you find her comely?'

'Whether I do or not, what is your meaning?'

'John tells me that she has been lonely since the death of her husband, and I believe that you have been lonely since the death of Mamma. If I were to wed John, would it not be a perfect arrangement for you to marry Martha?'

Thomas tutted. 'Is this your scheme, the two of you? To obtain our consent to your marriage at an unseemly age, by way of marrying us off to each other?'

'No, Dadda, I swear! It's just that, since we are so happy to have found each other, we would wish similar happiness for those who are dearest to us.'

'You have inherited your mother's wiles, I fear. But it would seem that I am destined to approach Martha regarding the prospect of your marrying John.'

'If you would be so good, Dadda. And perhaps you may find that there is some merit in my hopes for you and her. At least do not reject her out of hand, unless you intend to end your days as a lonely man who has never known the joys of union between a man and a woman.'

'I sincerely hope that you do not speak from experience,' Thomas muttered as he kissed her cheek and turned back down the hill.

There were two more arrivals from England shortly thereafter. The first was the *Sparrow*, a converted fishing barque that carried only eight passengers, led by Thomas Weston, who brought a stern message for the Plymouth congregation. The Merchant Adventurers whom he represented were far from content with the returns on their early investments, particularly after the *Fortune* had failed to sail back into her home port and was believed to have been seized and plundered by privateers.

Weston had been ordered by his masters to bring out a more sturdy and commercially minded group of men, who would establish a new colony dedicated to the acquisition of furs that they would either trap for themselves, or trade for with the natives. They spent barely two weeks in Plymouth, ignoring all invitations to partake in divine worship, and then set off by ship's cutter to the land to the north, where they established a new colony. They named it Weymouth when advised that the native name for the spot they had chosen was Wessagusset. It was in an area of land that traditionally belonged to a native tribe called the Massachusett, who were constantly engaged in guerilla warfare with the Wampanoag natives at Pokanoket, the home village of Massasoit.

Once they had assured themselves of the basic necessities for survival, two of the Wessagusset colonists, the brothers Gabriel and Morton Wheldon, approached Chief Massasoit with a request for native women to become their wives. Word drifted back to Plymouth of what had taken place, and opinion was divided among those attending meetings there regarding the wisdom of such a step, since it exposed Weymouth to attack from the Massachusetts once the white colonists made such a clear alliance with the Wampanoag. Standish insisted on training a band of men who could be sent to the defence of Weymouth if required.

Thomas took the contrary view that the men of Weymouth should have the freedom to make their own decisions, but should also be required to answer for the consequences. In vain he pointed out that Plymouth had insufficient arms to defend even itself, and that it would be a dangerous waste of resources to offer to defend another colony. He also pointed out that the decision to take native women for wives was a natural response from men who had journeyed halfway across the world without women. This earned a scornful response from Standish that desires of the flesh were a sign of weakness, and that true men should suppress them.

16

'Have you come for more stitching?' Martha Ford asked as Thomas appeared in the doorway of her hut. 'I can hardly conceive that you might be looking for your daughter, since you have never taken the trouble to call upon her here in the past.'

'Are you chastising me over my inadequacy as a parent?' Thomas asked, bristling.

Martha's face softened. 'Forgive my manners; they grow somewhat sharp of late. Please come inside and let me admire my handiwork now that it must have lost most of its surrounding bruises. Joanna is not here, as you can observe for yourself.' Martha nodded to the only chair in the hut.

Thomas shook his head politely. 'It is the only chair you have, and it is fitting that you occupy it. Has John not offered to make you others?'

'He no doubt would, had he the time,' Martha replied stiffly, 'but you seem intent on filling his days with tree felling. On the few occasions when I set eyes upon him, he seems to be on the point of exhaustion.'

'There is much to be done in that regard,' Thomas confirmed, 'since Selector Standish is determined to see our palisade completed before there can be any further native attacks.'

'Does he perceive that there will be?'

'I cannot speak for him, but for myself I would doubt it.'

'Let us not prevaricate, Master Bailey. You did not come here to discuss such things.'

'Please call me Thomas.'

'I will, should you so wish, but please do not presume from that to call me Martha. Such familiarity should perhaps be delayed until we become better acquainted through marriage.'

'You refer to the fondness that seems to have arisen between my daughter and your son?'

'What other marriage could there be, unless we are foolish enough to give in to those wild fantasies entertained by our respective offspring that we should be thus united?'

'You are obviously aware of their schemes,' Thomas mumbled.

'They have spoken of them, certainly,' Martha told him. 'John, on the rare occasions when he visits his widowed mother, and Joanna almost without ceasing. But she tells me that you are not a man for marriage. Does that mean that you simply took advantage of her mother?'

Thomas's face went bright red. 'Do I strike you as one who would take advantage of a young woman's foolishness?'

'So you consider it foolish that Joanna finds my son an attractive marriage prospect?'

'I feel that we will get on better if you cease twisting my words, as seems to be your delight. I said merely that her mother never succeeded in concealing her true feelings. I regard that as a sign of purity and honesty, and I will no more have you besmirch her memory that I will tolerate your suggestion that Joanna is too liberal with her favours.'

It fell silent for a moment, then Martha's previously stern expression relaxed. 'Forgive me — it is hard for me to discuss such matters without needing to steel myself against the grief that I still feel over the loss of my husband of some twenty-five years. I married him when I was not much older than Joanna, and those memories are still the most precious I possess. Seeing your daughter possessed of similar feelings only serves to deepen the wounds.'

'I am sorry that she should be the cause of such anguish on your part, although I feel sure that it is not intentional.'

'And with that I agree. You can be proud of the way you have raised her, Thomas. She is a credit to you, and a bright hope for the future of this colony. I could not wish for a better match for my son.'

'But should we be seen to encourage it, given their youth and inexperience?'

'If you have ever been in love, then you will know that there is no denying it. And the more something is forbidden, the greater the desire to engage in it.'

'I can only rely on your experience in such matters,' Thomas conceded.

'So you have never been in love?'

'Of course, but it was too late for me to act upon it, since the object of that love died before I was aware of the depth of my feelings.'

'Joanna's mother?'

Thomas nodded, unwilling to speak in case he choked on the tears that he could feel welling up.

Martha seemed to perceive his struggle. 'Would you deny such wonderful feelings to our son and daughter?'

Thomas was inclined to challenge her choice of phrase, but just then there was a faint cry coming from a box in the corner.

Martha rose swiftly to her feet. 'That must be young Martha. If she requires feeding, you will have to grant me some privacy.'

Unsure of what to do, Thomas held back for the moment, and watched as Martha took the small girl out of her wrappings and stood her on the earth floor, where she wobbled uncertainly, then sat down heavily on her bottom.

'Why do you smile?' Martha asked Thomas. 'Do not attempt to tell me that she looks like her mother, because all children look the same at this age.'

'It's just that she reminds me of Joanna at that age,' Thomas mumbled as he watched the small girl's attempts to place one leg in front of the other. 'She will soon be walking.'

'What makes you think so?' Martha asked.

Thomas nodded at the child's movements. 'She has the instincts, just as Joanna did. Let us see if she is ready.'

He moved forward a few feet, then knelt on the ground and held out his arms. He instructed Martha to let go of the infant, and she first tottered, then made a dash for Thomas's open arms, into which she landed with a triumphant squeak. Thomas held her tightly and kissed the top of her head as tears of remembrance rolled down his face.

Martha chuckled. 'Clearly you have done this before. You are a natural father — and little Martha seems to have enjoyed having one, albeit for a brief period. Let our children follow their instincts, Thomas. Do please call again soon, and then you may call me Martha.'

Thomas walked back to his hut in a daze. A vision of Martha's warm smile, her flowing black hair and her deep blue eyes seemed to precede him, and he almost walked past his hut. John sat on the ground outside and eyed him curiously.

'You have just called on my mother? What had she to say?'

'Perhaps, if you visited her more often, you wouldn't need to use me as a messenger,' Thomas replied with mock severity. He nodded at the pile of timber lying by the doorpost. 'If I instruct Master Adams to show you how to measure accurately, and make secure joints between adjacent pieces of wood, do you think you could make a chair?'

'I would be willing to try, if it means that I shall not be called upon to fell trees this day,' John replied with a grin. 'But do we not have enough chairs? Or is it your intention that we make one to exchange for something else?'

'If you visited your mother as often as your duty requires, you might be aware that she has only one chair. It is necessary for those visiting her to stand.'

'In truth she has very few visitors, or so she complains to me,' John replied.

'And what about the object of your affections? My daughter Joanna? Must she sit on a damp earthen floor every day? If you do not feel inspired to create something for your mother, then think of it as a labour of love for Joanna.'

'You do not disapprove of my attentions towards her?'

'Not at present, but be well warned: if you do or say anything to upset her, or if you abuse her innocence in any way, I will make a hole in your head that even your mother couldn't sew back together. Now, set about making that chair.'

The next vessel to arrive in Plymouth was able to tie up at the crude jetty that had been built out into the bay. She was called the *Anne*, and to everyone's delight she was followed by the *Little James*, bearing much-needed supplies. Standish had by now established a small militia made up of young men, one of whom was John Ford. They eagerly unloaded the muskets, bags of powder and cases of shot balls, and from dawn to dusk the embryonic army could be seen parading up and down the open ground in front of the Meeting Room.

This left Thomas without John's services for tree felling, but he was fortunate to find several strong young men among the ninety incoming settlers on board the *Anne,* not all of whom had come out in pursuit of religious freedom, and within days the crash of falling timber could once again be heard from the forest. Much of that timber was loaded below decks on the two vessels sent out by the Merchant Adventurers Company, along with beaver furs, and it was anticipated that the sponsors back in London would be encouraged to send fresh supplies in return.

Standish's insistence on a fourth side to the palisade, facing towards the bay, meant that Plymouth now resembled a military fortress. Squanto and his companions noted this during their visits, and they warned Governor Bradford that the settlement at Wessagusset continued to be an annoyance to the Massachusett tribe, and that there were signs that war parties were being prepared to launch an attack on the colonists there.

Standish began to plague the Council with requests to take a contingent from his militia south to Wessagusset — or 'Weymouth', as the settlers called it — in a show of force to deter any native attack. His main opponent was Thomas, who argued that it was bad enough having strong young men diverted from worthwhile manual labour in order to defend Plymouth against an attack that might never happen. Sending some of them to Wessagusset, he claimed, was an extravagance that the colony could not afford.

Thomas's shoulder injury had not yet healed enough for him to be able to swing an axe. He had tried only once and had reopened the scar tissue. John had taken one look at the blood on Thomas's shirt and slipped silently to his mother's hut. He had then taken Joanna for an evening stroll along the foreshore, advising her of her father's difficulty. She had rushed to his hut and persuaded him to allow her to dress the gaping wound, after washing it with water from the bay, threatening that if he did not, she would summon Martha Ford with her needles. Thomas had grumbled about being held to ransom by a girl of fourteen, but he had nevertheless submitted to her nursing with grimaces and moans of misery as the saltwater bit into the reopened wound.

His experience had taught him to be patient, particularly after a handful of strong and eager men arrived on the *Anne*, whom he claimed for a labour force before Standish could recruit them. Thomas was seated on a tree stump, supervising their actions when he became aware of a small group heading his way up the gentle slope from the settlement. After a short while he recognised Joanna, John and Martha, carrying little Martha in her arms, and he stood up to welcome them.

Joanna reached him first and held out a small parcel covered by a cloth. 'Martha was taught how to bake on an open fire, and she made these berry tarts for you. As you'll deduce, she's a very able cook.'

Thomas thanked her, leaned down to kiss her cheek, then looked up enquiringly at Martha and John, who had caught up with her. 'Thank you most gratefully for these tarts, Mistress Ford, but are they so valuable that my daughter required an escort to bring them up here?'

Martha smiled. 'It's "Martha" to you, and we have need of your consent to something.'

'That "something" being what, precisely?' Thomas asked suspiciously.

Joanna took his hand and looked pleadingly into his eyes. 'John and I wish to approach the meeting for their permission to become betrothed, and we are told that our parents must give their consent. Martha has already agreed to do so, and so…'

'And so you thought you'd come up here and bribe me with sweetmeats?'

'Well, yes,' Joanna admitted.

Thomas transferred his gaze to John. 'You are still numbered among the armed band?'

'Indeed I am, but we have not been drilling as regularly as we previously did. Master Standish has fresh interests to occupy him.'

'What could possibly have diverted Myles Standish from playing the part of the brave warrior?' Thomas asked.

'Barbara Dowling,' Martha told him. 'She came off the *Anne* bearing a letter of introduction from someone among those who have financed this colony. It seems that she is skilled in the matter of herbs, since her father is an apothecary in London. But she is also most comely, with long fair hair, and she and Master Standish have been seen walking, sometimes hand in hand.'

Thomas gave a hollow laugh. 'Master Standish once told me that military men should not be distracted from their duties by a wife and family. It seems that the man is possessed of a forked tongue, if he is now contemplating taking another wife. He has been a widower for less than two years.'

'He merely walks alongside her, occasionally holding her hand,' Joanna pointed out.

'As you do with John?' Thomas teased. 'Indeed, it is to be hoped that the two of you do nothing more, yet you regard yourselves sufficiently qualified to seek permission for a betrothal?'

'If you could see your way clear to granting your permission for that,' John added eagerly, 'I will make it my business to prove my manhood to all and sundry, and leave you in no doubt that I am more than capable of looking after a wife and children.'

'And a mother, it is to be hoped,' Thomas replied, nodding in Martha's direction. 'Or is it part of your great scheme that another man must undertake *her* protection?'

'If one can ward off danger with needles, then I need no protection from any man,' Martha told him. 'But husbands are required for a great many purposes, are they not?'

On the following meeting day, Joanna and John stood nervously in the front rank of the congregation. When the point in the service was reached for announcements, John requested that those assembled give their blessing for his betrothal to Mistress Bailey. William Bradford looked at Thomas with raised eyebrows, and Thomas responded with a barely perceptible nod. Bradford then asked, 'Have the parents consented?'

'I have given my consent for John Ford,' Martha called out strongly.

'And I for Joanna Bailey,' Thomas responded.

'That being the case, does anyone know of any impediment to such a betrothal?' Bradford asked. When there were none, he smiled and announced, 'That being the case, I invite the congregation to join hands and give consent in the appropriate manner.'

Martha stepped from John's side and slipped behind him to occupy the space on Thomas's right, taking his hand.

Thomas was aware that Squanto had been in the settlement for some days, but he had no inkling of what his business might be until summoned to a meeting of selectors. Standish scowled as he saw Thomas joining the group.

167

'Pay no attention to whatever peaceful drivel this man may preach at you,' he said, glowering in Thomas's direction. 'The matter is an urgent one, and must be addressed before the enemy have time to strike.'

'You clearly have the advantage of me,' Thomas remarked drily as he took his seat on the long wooden bench. 'Are we about to come under attack?'

'Not we — the settlement at Weymouth,' Standish told him. 'Squanto warns us that the Massachusett warriors have moved down through the forests so as to be little more than a league from the village, and he fears that they are preparing to attack.'

'If he is that certain of his information, why does he not offer to protect the colonists himself?' Thomas asked suspiciously.

'If Master Bailey knew as much about native politics as he does about tree felling, then he would be aware that if Squanto and his warriors take up arms against the Massachusett warriors, he commits his Pokanoket people to all-out war with them, with no certainty that the remainder of the Wampanoag confederacy will support them.'

Thomas remained unconvinced, and argued strongly that Plymouth should not involve itself in the affairs of Weymouth. But his was almost a lone voice, and he stalked angrily back to his hut, where he found Joanna sitting outside, talking to John.

'Have you been discussing Master Standish's bold plan to defend Weymouth?' John asked eagerly.

Thomas screwed up his face in distaste. 'He's persuaded the Council to approve his ill-considered proposal. Why do you ask? Hopefully you are not going to add your arm to such an ill-considered venture?'

'I'm a member of his trained band,' John reminded him proudly, 'and if he orders us to travel south, then I'm sworn to follow his command.'

'You begin to sound as pompous and vainglorious as him,' Thomas snorted, then he turned to Joanna. 'Whatever powers of persuasion you possess over this idiot, employ them in order to dissuade him from following Standish to what may be his death.'

'Surely this is John's great opportunity to prove his worth to the colony, that we may be married all the sooner?' she said.

Thomas's face grew pale as he took both her hands and looked sternly into her eyes. 'A man may show his worth to his fellows without risking his life in unwise, and totally unnecessary, warfare. I have never done so — do you therefore regard me as less of a man?'

'Of course not, Dadda,' she reassured him. 'But John wishes to establish himself this way, and I am surely bound to support him in whatever he does.'

'Hopefully it won't come to pass,' Thomas muttered as he pushed past them into his hut. 'But when you kiss John goodnight, ask yourself whether it may be for the last time.'

Two days later, the trained band were summoned to the centre of the Plymouth parade ground and issued with their muskets, bayonets, and their first round of powder and shot. Thomas angrily withdrew to his hut with muttered oaths as he saw them marching down the foreshore to where the ship's cutter was bobbing on the incoming tide, waiting to carry them south. A few moments later he heard a familiar voice calling his name, and he stepped outside.

Martha was wringing her apron in her hands. 'Thomas, save our son — please!'

'From what? His own foolishness? He's *your* son, anyway — no son of mine would be so foolish.'

'When he marries Joanna, he'll be our son, and do not try to pretend that you do not care what happens to him. Please, Thomas!'

'What does Joanna say?'

'She's just a foolish girl with no real idea of what John has got himself into. But I do, and I fear for his life.'

'Do you not also fear for mine, should I go after him?'

'Of course, and should you both return alive, I will show you how important you are to me. But for the time being, I fear that John will get himself killed. He needs the wisdom of the man he looks upon as his new father at his elbow. Do you wish to see us lose a son, and Joanna a husband?'

'Of course not, and if it will ease your mind, I'll add my name to those whose arrogant stupidity has led them thus far. Should I not return, let it be known that this business was not of my making.'

Martha stepped forward and kissed him warmly on the lips, and Thomas could taste her tears as she whispered, 'Should you not return, I shall also lose the best man I could have wished to marry. Now, lose no more time — the boat is still drawn up on the shingle.'

Thomas dashed into his hut and grabbed his cloak and musket, hoping that others could supply him with the shot and powder. He then raced down towards the shore, calling out, 'Wait for me!'

Standish was standing in the bow, and he raised his eyebrows as he saw Thomas racing towards him. He ordered the helmsman to delay pushing off until the latest arrival could clamber into the cutter.

'You have had second thoughts, it would seem,' Standish crowed. 'You now wish to join our glorious enterprise?'

'No,' John replied angrily, 'I am sent to preserve the life of my daughter's intended. You can waste yours, should you wish, but my best endeavours will be directed towards the *saving* of life, rather than its wanton squandering. So order the boatman to push off, and let's get this over with!'

17

They alighted from the boat and moved along the shoreline some leagues short of the Weymouth settlement. Standish insisted on leading the way, and imposed total silence on the fifteen members of his trained band who had volunteered to accompany him as they located a well-worn forest track that had probably first been made by native tribes many years ago.

Three hours later they smelled smoke, and Standish raised a hand to indicate that they should halt; a second signal waved them all down to ground level. As they knelt silently in the undergrowth behind him, he crept forward. Finally he raised himself upright, turned and whispered, 'The smoke is coming from a camp up ahead. I think it may be Weymouth, so be on your guard!'

Several minutes later, he waved his men out into a broad semi-circle, then gave the signal to move forward. 'Why are we creeping up on our fellow colonists?' John whispered to Thomas.

'Probably because we can't be certain that the natives haven't overtaken them already, and are lying in wait for us,' Thomas suggested.

As they pushed noiselessly through the final line of trees that fringed the crude settlement, with their muskets primed and held at waist height, the only sight that greeted them was of lazy open fires and white men digging listlessly. Standish raised his hand and they all halted, listening for a shout of native challenge. But the voice that called out to them was decidedly English, and more inquisitive than aggressive.

'Are we under attack, or being taken prisoner, or what, exactly?' A bedraggled man with an unkempt beard had emerged from the worst constructed hut that Thomas had ever seen.

'Who might you be?' Standish demanded.

'I was about to ask you the same thing,' the man called back. 'You some of them Godly types from up north?'

'I'm Myles Standish, Captain of the Plymouth Militia, and we're here to preserve you from a native attack.'

'Really?' the man asked with some amusement. 'Has my mother-in-law been complaining because I got her daughter with child again? I'm Gabe Wheldon, and I'm what passes for the top man around these parts. Welcome to Weymouth — and to be perfectly honest, you're *very* welcome to it!'

'You've seen nothing of any native raiding parties?' Standish asked as he waved for his men to lower their weapons.

Wheldon shook his head. 'The only natives we see come down here to trade furs for the grog we make out of tree bark. Speaking of which, step inside and we'll show you some hospitality, since you've obviously come a long way for nothing.'

Standish was waved into the hut from which Wheldon had recently emerged. He turned and beckoned for Thomas to accompany him, after ordering his men to sit on the ground around the small settlement, but to keep their eyes and ears open, and their weapons primed. Thomas stepped into the gloom of the hut, which smelled of highly spiced meat. As his eyes adjusted, they lit upon a native woman who was breastfeeding a child. There was a pot boiling in the centre of the hut which, since it had no roof vent, was rapidly filling with the fumes from whatever was cooking.

Wheldon invited them to take a set on the earthen floor, then nodded towards the woman with the child. 'That's my woman — I call her "Nancy". Now, let's have something strong to drink, shall we? This year's is a lot better than last year's, and we get a better exchange for it from the natives.'

Both Standish and Thomas hastily declined, and suggested that perhaps they might be better able to conduct a conversation if they sat outside. They moved out into the early dusk while Standish repeated the warning they'd received from Squanto regarding the gathering of the Massachusett warriors in the forest to their south. Wheldon shook his head in disbelief.

'That doesn't make any sense. We do a nice trade with the native tribes, and they seem to have formed a liking for our grog, so why would they attack us?'

'They've given no sign that they resent you settling their land?' Thomas asked.

Again, Wheldon shook his head. 'Why would they? It's worth nothing. There are only a few mangy animals wandering about — a few less since we learned how to cook and eat them — and if there's gold or suchlike to be found in these parts, we've yet to find it.'

'Have you not organised any defences?' Standish asked as he looked in vain for any stockade walls.

Wheldon laughed. 'Against what? Like I said, the native tribes are friendly, and the last wild boar that wandered in here finished up in the pot.'

Standish shook his head in frustration. 'As far as I can tell, your settlement is wide open to attack, and you're just assuming that the natives who surround you are going to remain friendly.'

'They have done so far,' said Wheldon, 'so like I said, you've had a wasted journey, unless you want to trade some of your firearms for grog.'

'We'll be doing nothing of the sort,' Standish told him stiffly, 'and we won't be leaving until I'm thoroughly satisfied that you're under no threat from the surrounding natives. Tell me, who's their leader, or at least the man you do business with?'

'That'll be Obtakiest,' Wheldon replied grudgingly. 'He's the local chief, or so Nancy reckons. She's the only one who can talk to him, and he's the one we trade with, although he's normally accompanied by a couple of strong men with spears, bows and arrows and the likes.'

Standish looked thoughtful for a moment. 'I'd like to meet with this local chief you describe, with your woman as the interpreter. I need to impress upon him that if he and his warriors make any attempt to attack this settlement, they'll have me and my trained band to deal with. How does that sound to you?'

Wheldon shrugged dismissively. 'Can't do any harm, I suppose. When do you want to talk to him?'

'As soon as possible, so that we can then all be on our way. Do you have a hut we can use for the meeting, and could your woman prepare a meal?'

'Of course. I'll get a message sent to Obtakiest right away — there's a native boy who does odd jobs around the place. I'll get him to invite the chief to come in for a feast and a trading meeting tomorrow, around the middle of the day.'

'Be sure to emphasise that we come in peace, and that he need not bring a heavily armed escort with him. We just want to conduct talks regarding future trade.'

Once he was alone with Standish, Thomas asked, 'Why should we concern ourselves over future trade between this place and the natives?'

Standish smiled. 'It will be a little more than that, you'll see. I wish to send a message to the Massachusett tribe that it would not be in their best interests to clash with white settlers with muskets. When they see what we're capable of, these people will be free from any future threats — not that they seem to deserve our intervention on their behalf.'

There was something about his manner that made Thomas highly suspicious. Once Standish had risen to his feet, walked over to where the men under his command were seated and instructed them that they could relax for the rest of the day, Thomas beckoned John over to him and lowered his voice.

'I don't trust Standish's motives. Something tells me to keep well back from what he's planning on doing when he meets with a local native chief tomorrow, so stay by my side. We'll make a pretence of guarding the hut where they hold the meeting. And speaking of huts, where are we supposed to sleep tonight?'

'Standish didn't say anything about that,' John told him. 'And until you mentioned a meeting tomorrow, I didn't even know that we would be staying here overnight. We were just told to take it easy for the rest of the day, and I'm hungry. How about you?'

'I'll see what I can arrange,' Thomas promised, then walked over to where Standish was sitting with the remainder of his trained band.

He looked up as Thomas approached. 'Was that you attempting to talk one of my men into deserting?'

'That man — as you will of course be aware — is betrothed to my daughter, and I was simply enquiring as to his welfare.

And now I make enquiry about the welfare of the rest of your private army. Have you made any provision for them to be fed and allocated somewhere to sleep overnight? If it comes to that, have you even advised them that they won't be leaving until tomorrow, when you complete your meeting with the local chief in order to demonstrate how powerful you are?'

'Is that right?' one of his men asked, amid the low grumblings of the remainder.

Standish shot Thomas a furious look. 'Don't be insubordinate! You volunteered to join this trained band for this expedition, and while you're part of it you'll answer to my orders, understand? I will obviously see to the matters of food and shelter, but I'll thank you to sit down and stop stirring things up.'

Rather than cause any more dissent, Thomas did as instructed. Later in the day, a girl wandered across to where the men were sitting and gave them a pot of gruel and several loaves of stale brown bread. She also nodded towards a hut that was leaning at a perilous angle and told them that they could shelter there, but that they'd need to make improvements to the roof in case it collapsed on them.

Thomas undertook to supervise the repairs, which took up most of the remainder of that day. The following morning, after a very uncomfortable night, the men were ordered to march up and down by Standish in what was presumably an attempt to keep them occupied while demonstrating their discipline to any natives who might be watching.

When the sun was at its highest, a large native man emerged from the trees to the south of the colony. He was flanked by two tall warriors carrying spears, with bows strung across their shoulders and arrow shafts protruding from sacks that were suspended from their waists. They were shown into the best hut in the settlement, and Nancy began serving them platters of fruit and portions of turkey that she had roasted over an open fire outside.

Thomas had persuaded Standish that the best service he could offer would be to stand guard outside the hut with John while Standish and three of his largest acolytes confronted the three visitors. Thomas kept an ear focused on the stilted conversation that was taking place between Standish and Obtakiest, via Nancy, on the subject of future trading. He could not see anything beyond what was revealed by the narrow entrance to the hut, but he gave John a low hiss of warning as he saw Standish's three henchmen reach inside their tunics for their bayonets, which they pointed at the earth floor.

'I fear some dreadful betrayal,' Thomas whispered, just as there was a cry of outrage. Through the doorway, Thomas saw bayonets being raised to waist height and two natives falling to the ground with agonised yells. Obtakiest fled the hut, yelling at the top of his voice.

From the trees skirting the settlement, a group of warriors answered the call. Standish was the next out of the hut, calling on his trained band to engage the incoming natives. Thomas grabbed John's arm and the two of them set off at breakneck speed through the undergrowth that fringed the woods, heading down the track by which they had first entered Weymouth.

They had barely gone a quarter of a mile before a second line of natives rose up from the undergrowth on either side of the track ahead of them, and Thomas urged John to keep running. As they panted past the waiting natives, four of them could be seen inserting arrows into their bowstrings. Thomas heard a cry of pain from John, who was a few yards behind him, and he turned in time to see the youth falling to the ground.

Thomas turned back to stand over John. An arrow was deeply embedded in his thigh, and blood was seeping through his breeches. Thomas raised the bayonet that he'd been hiding in the folds of his jacket, waving it menacingly at three men, who loaded their bows and pointed their arrows at his chest. He was in the process of saying a mental farewell to Joanna and Martha Ford when he heard the call of a young woman, and the natives by whom he was surrounded lowered their bows.

A young native woman approached them, who looked familiar to Thomas. She smiled at him and called out, 'Peace, you said — go in peace. Now you go free, with your debt repaid.'

Thomas suddenly remembered where he'd seen her before. He'd been felling timber during his first few weeks in the colony, and she'd broken from her hiding place. He could recall lowering his musket just before she'd emerged. Thanking God for his forbearance on that occasion, Thomas raised his hand in greeting. 'I'm going back to the boat,' he told the woman. 'I carry my son, who was wounded by an arrow.'

He reached down for John, heaved him across his shoulder, and set off down the track towards where they'd left the cutter the previous day, not daring to look behind him. After an hour, he stopped to catch his breath and lowered John gently to the ground. There was no sign of anyone in pursuit.

Thomas looked down at John, whose face was ashen, his breath coming in hoarse rasps. 'How are you managing?' he asked.

'It hurts like I've never hurt before,' John replied, 'but just leave me here, and I'll wait for the others. You can't carry me all the way back.'

'Can I not? Do you think that either Joanna or your mother would thank me for abandoning you here, just as the dusk is setting in? And what makes you think that the others will survive the massacre that Standish has brought down on their heads? Conserve your energy, for we have a long journey ahead of us, and you may have to hop for some of it.'

It was getting dark, and Thomas thought that wild beasts might be stalking the forest track, no doubt drawn by the smell of the blood from John's wound. He realised that their best chance of survival was to regain the shoreline, where hopefully the boat would still be awaiting the return of Standish's men, although there would now be only Thomas and the boatman to row it.

There were stealthy noises from the undergrowth on either side of them as Thomas staggered on, struggling with John's weight on his shoulder. Suddenly the ground became more sloping, and Thomas felt his boots sliding in what felt like mud. There was also a lapping sound that could only be coming from small waves, and with a shout of triumph he realised that they had made it back safely to the bay. A hoarse call of challenge reached his ears from a hundred yards downstream, and he lowered John gently onto the shingle as he staggered forward.

Thomas checked the pan of his musket for powder, then crunched along the shoreline to where he could just make out the outline of the cutter. A cautious face rose above the gunnels and a voice called out, 'Who's that?'

'It's only me — Thomas Bailey,' Thomas called back.

'Where are the rest of you?' the boatman demanded.

Thomas thought quickly. 'They were wiped out in an ambush. I have a wounded man lying back there, and we have to get back to Plymouth without delay.'

'I don't know about that,' the boatman replied. 'I take my orders from Captain Standish.'

Thomas walked steadily towards the boat and raised his musket. 'From now on, you take your orders from the end of my musket. Now, bring the boat further down the beach and help me get the wounded man on board.'

Ten minutes later John was lying in the scuppers of the boat, and Thomas persuaded the boatman that between them they could follow the shoreline north, rowing steadily towards Plymouth. The boat was a heavily built thirty-foot ship's cutter that would normally be powered by four or six men. By the time the two of them slid it up the beach at Plymouth it was the middle of another day, and the sweat was pouring down both their faces.

There was a challenge from a man on the rampart behind the palisade, and Thomas called up for assistance. Ten minutes later he was thanking the boatman for his efforts, and willing hands were carrying the now unconscious John towards Martha's hut. Thomas sat down heavily in the middle of the square and muttered his thanks to God for their safe delivery as he heard Martha's screams.

'What happened to Dadda?' Joanna cried.

'Over here!' Thomas called out with his remaining breath.

Joanna scampered across the square and threw herself onto the ground to embrace him. 'What happened? Are you wounded?'

'Not wounded — exhausted. Help me to my feet and across to my hut.'

Thomas slept for almost two days, for some of which he was delirious. He was visited several times by Joanna, bearing food and beer, and by Martha, bearing tearful thanks. She told him that the arrow had been removed from John's leg and that she had sewn it up. John was weak but was expected to live, and Martha believed Thomas to be the bravest man on God's earth.

He was vaguely aware that Standish and half his men had returned from Weymouth some days after he had staggered back. Eventually, Governor Bradford appeared in his hut doorway, accompanied by two of the trained band armed with muskets.

'I detest having to do this to an old friend, Thomas, but I have to convey you to the prison hut to await trial by the meeting.'

'On what charges?'

'Cowardice, desertion, mutiny, and conduct likely to endanger the colony. Standish is out to have you expelled from Plymouth, and if what he alleges is true, then I'm not sure that I can save you.'

18

The appointed day of the trial arrived. Thomas was led from the prison hut that he had occupied for two days, while Joanna had tearfully brought him food and drink prepared by her and Martha.

The Meeting Room was filled to capacity, and the only ones seated were Governor Bradford and the selectors who flanked him on either side, and who would be delivering the final verdict. Only one man had been expelled from the Plymouth colony thus far, his offence being 'lewd and libidinous conduct' after over-consumption of crude liquor distilled in his hut. His body had been discovered in the forest several weeks later, half eaten by wild animals.

Thomas had been one of the selectors whose majority verdict had cast the man off to fend for himself. The irony was not lost on him as he stood silently awaiting the commencement of the proceedings, occasionally gazing round at the walls that he had helped to erect almost three years previously. He was not restrained in any way, for he had sworn on the Bible to make no attempt to escape, but on either side of him stood surviving members of the trained band who had been part of the expedition to Weymouth. They could probably have testified the truth of what had happened there, were they not sworn to obey Standish in everything. Today, their duty was to make a grab for Thomas if he broke his holy oath.

Governor Bradford looked ill at ease, and the rapidly ageing William Brewster looked sick at the prospect of deciding the fate of the man he had first employed two decades ago. The remaining five selectors all wore expressions of dread as Governor Bradford invited Captain Myles Standish to bring his charges.

Thomas listened in disbelief, but maintained a dignified silence, as Standish recounted how he had been negotiating with a native chief for the ongoing safety and friendship of a fellow Christian settlement when he and his small party had been attacked without warning, and had been forced to defend themselves. At this point, he alleged, Thomas Bailey had deserted, dragging along with him his prospective son-in-law John Ford, against whom could be levelled no accusation, since he had been overborne by Thomas's strength. No mention was made of the fact that the need to flee had been the result of Standish's unprovoked and treacherous slaughter of two native men, nor was it suggested that Thomas's subsequent actions had been motivated by the need to preserve the life of a young man whose impending marriage would ensure the birth of new souls to boost the size of the community.

Standish then claimed that Thomas had commandeered, at gunpoint, the cutter that was the only means of escape for the trained band who had been forced to fight their way out of the ambush. As a result, their return had been by land, hacking their way through an overgrown and perilous track through the forest. They finally reached Plymouth with only half the men they had set out with, leaving wives and mothers to be advised of the fate to which Thomas Bailey had consigned them.

Thomas wondered whether any of the remaining members of the trained band had been bribed or bullied into corroborating Standish's twisted version of events. Bradford raised a hand and indicated that he had a few questions to pose in response to the account that they had just heard.

'When this meeting commenced with the native chief — the one that ended in bloodshed — were you armed?' he asked Standish.

'Of course, Governor, since the natives who attended were also armed.'

'And where were the rest of your trained band?'

'Outside the hut in which the meeting took place.'

'Where, in particular, was Master Bailey?'

'Immediately outside the hut, allegedly keeping guard, as he had volunteered to do, along with Master Ford.'

'When you were attacked by the natives, this was inside the hut?'

'Yes.'

'But it would seem from what you told us that Master Bailey made no attempt to come to your assistance?'

'That's correct, Governor. I never saw Master Bailey again once I entered that hut for the meeting with the natives.'

'So for all you knew, Thomas Bailey was one of those who fought off the attack from the natives who rushed into the settlement after the attempted murder of yourself and your three companions?'

'I was told later that he had run off at the first sign of any aggression towards ourselves.'

'By whom?'

'Master Philip Tench.'

'Will he be testifying before the meeting?'

'No, Governor — his was one of the bodies we were obliged to leave behind after the attack.'

Governor Bradford's face set as he pursued the point. 'Master Tench died during the confrontation between your trained band and the natives that emerged immediately after the attack on you inside the hut?'

'Yes, Governor.'

'And yet you would have us believe that during that brief, and highly fraught, period of time, he was able to advise you that Master Bailey had deserted?'

'It was indeed a fraught and hazardous moment, Governor, and I cannot now recall everything that was said, or at what precise moment.'

Bradford held his gaze for a moment, then leaned sideways to whisper something to William Brewster, who smiled, nodded, and looked considerably relieved.

The next to swear solemnly on the Bible was Josiah Temple, one of those members of the trained band who had been inside the hut with Standish. He looked nervously towards the seated elders before being invited to speak. Temple then recited, in a tone that reminded the listeners of a stage actor anxious not to forget his lines, how the conversation with the native chief had been proceeding unremarkably when those accompanying him had suddenly leapt up from the floor and set about the trained band with clubs. They had reacted by vanquishing their attackers with their bayonets, then pursuing the escaping chief out of the hut, where they had been set upon by a large number of warriors armed with spears and bows and arrows. They had fought their way free of them, abandoning some of their own dead and dying in the dust of Weymouth, then raced back down the track towards where they had left their boat, only to discover that it was no longer there. They had followed the shoreline north as far as was possible but had been obliged to take to the woodland tracks whenever outcrops of rock had made further progress down the beach impossible. Eventually Plymouth had come into view behind the headland that formed the southern arm of the bay in which it lay. Unable to reach it directly, the colonists had been forced back into the forest, to re-enter Plymouth via a woodland track in the middle of the third day after their flight.

Temple was about to walk away, but once again Bradford began to ask questions.

'You say that you were attacked inside the meeting hut by natives armed with clubs?'

'Yes, Governor.'

'Taken totally by surprise?'

'Correct.'

'But you set about them with your bayonets and prevailed?'

'Also correct.'

'Why were your bayonets not attached to your muskets, which I believe to be their normal location?'

'We'd been ordered to remove them and conceal them in our cloaks.'

'By whom?'

'By Captain Standish. He was the only one with the authority to command such an action.'

'Did he indicate that he was expecting an act of treachery from the natives?'

'No, Governor.'

'Did no-one see fit to question why he was giving you the order to have your bayonets at the ready?'

'One does not question Captain Standish's orders, Governor.'

Bradford and Brewster raised their eyebrows, and Temple was allowed to stand down.

The third and final witness was Amos Bellamy, the boatswain from the *Anne* who had been in command of the cutter. Governor Bradford had only one question for him.

'When Master Bailey ordered you to bring the boat back to Plymouth, did he give you any indication of why he was accompanied only by Master Ford?'

'Yes, he told me that the rest of the trained band had perished.'

They had reached the middle of the day, and the proceedings were adjourned for one hour. Thomas was brought some beer and a handful of berry tarts that Martha had cooked, and which Joanna, with one of her winning smiles, had carried past the guard beside the prison door. Thomas made a pretence of eating and drinking out of politeness, but he was almost choking in anticipation of the ordeal that lay ahead. The meeting resumed, and he was obliged to give his version of events.

He did so hesitatingly at first, but he warmed up when describing how he had witnessed the murderous and unprovoked attack on the natives by Standish's men. He only began to falter when describing how he had ordered John to run when the remaining natives had attacked Weymouth, for which they could hardly be blamed in the circumstances. He paused for a moment to collect his thoughts, and Bradford took the opportunity to ask a question.

'Some might say that this was cowardice on your part, to run from an enemy about to engage you?'

'That depends upon your definition of cowardice,' Thomas argued back. 'I had just seen a foul piece of treachery by Captain Standish, who in my estimation is not fit to lead a cow into pasture, let alone a company of men into battle.' He paused for the laughter that this provoked, mainly from members of Standish's own trained band — a point noted with grim satisfaction by Bradford as he ordered silence. Then he nodded for Thomas to continue.

'One of the attributes of good leadership is to know when a battle is lost, and to preserve the lives that remain,' said Thomas. 'It seemed to me, in the few seconds that I had available, that we were outnumbered, and that a swift retreat would be the best course. The only man next to me was John Ford, and so I pulled him with me as I ran.'

'Even though you had no authority to give orders to the trained band?'

'He is also my daughter's intended, and I felt that I owed it to her to preserve his life.'

'And he was subsequently wounded during your attempted escape?'

'Yes, Governor. He suffered an arrow in his leg, and it was left to me to bring him home safely.'

'You do not deny commandeering the boat at the point of your musket?'

'No, Governor. We were both on the point of expiry through exhaustion, and it was our only way back to Plymouth.'

'It was also the only way back for the others, was it not?'

'Indeed, but I truly believed that they could not have survived the native retaliation.'

'So you did not lie to the boatman Bellamy? You merely told him what you genuinely believed to be the truth?'

'That's correct, Governor.'

'Is there anything further you wish to add, or any other witness you wish to call?'

'No further witnesses, but I would like to add that when I consider my actions again, I believe that I was wrong in commandeering the boat.'

'But if you again found yourself in the state of mind in which you did so, would your actions be any different?'

'I would like to believe that they would, but in all honesty, I cannot say that.'

Thomas was relieved to have been able to convey his account without giving vent to the cold rage that he felt regarding Standish's cowardly actions. He was also profoundly depressed by the realisation that his actions regarding the boat had been selfish and hot-headed.

The elders had announced that they would consider the matter overnight and give their ruling at noon the following day. Governor Bradford was admitted to the prison hut that Thomas was still occupying alone, bearing cooked slices of meat, a freshly baked loaf and a flagon of beer. He lowered himself onto the ground alongside the narrow pallet and looked Thomas in the eye.

'You and I have been friends since boyhood, Thomas, so I will be honest with you. The meeting is highly sceptical of the version of events narrated by Myles Standish and is inclined to give you the benefit of the doubt. They are also highly impressed by your courage and determination in bringing John Ford back to safety against all odds. But that is as far as we can go in your favour.'

Thomas nodded sadly. 'It's the matter of my actions regarding the boat, is it not?'

'I'm afraid so. You no doubt, in your own mind, had good reason to believe that there would be no other survivors. However, there were, so while we can easily dismiss any suggestion of cowardice or mutiny, there can be no doubt that your actions placed the lives of other settlers in jeopardy. We are obliged to rule against you on that charge.'

'So will I be expelled from Plymouth?' Thomas asked.

Bradford smiled. 'It will come down to the decision of the meeting as a whole. The elders have the authority to decide guilt or innocence, but only the meeting can determine your fate.'

'Then my only hope is that there are enough people who have such a good opinion of me that they will allow me to remain among them,' Thomas concluded.

'And that you may safely leave with me,' said Bradford. 'I bid you goodnight.'

After Bradford had left, Thomas heard a brief conversation between a man and a woman at the entrance to the prison hut. The next moment, he was looking up at Martha Ford.

'I was fortunate that your guard was prepared to look the other way in return for a handful of my berry tarts,' she said. 'Now, move over.'

'I beg your pardon?' Thomas replied in amazement as he saw her slip her gown down to the dusty floor.

'Move over,' she repeated. 'It's a cold night, so slide that cover aside and let me under it with you.'

'But you are naked. If you join me in here, it may lead to sin,' Thomas objected.

Martha chuckled. 'If we do not sin this night, Thomas Bailey, then my visit will have been in vain.'

19

The Meeting Room was less crowded the following morning, since the only ones allowed in were those who were members by virtue of their religious observances. Nevertheless, the air was hot and heavy, and Thomas felt sweat trickling down his back as he stood facing those who were about to deliver their pronouncement. This was not, however, what was dominating his thoughts, since Bradford had already intimated what was about to follow. Instead, Thomas was preoccupied with the memory of the previous night, and the realisation that he had wasted years by not taking a wife.

Governor Bradford looked Thomas in the eye and announced the verdict. 'Thomas Bailey, we have duly considered those matters that were brought before us, and have prayed to God that he put into our heads the true and just outcome. We do not find it proven that you were guilty of cowardice, insubordination or treasonous actions against the Colony of Plymouth. However, it is our considered judgment, arrived at with considerable regret and heart-searching, that by forcibly taking command of the vessel that was waiting to bring the trained band back to Plymouth, you were guilty of endangering life. This exposes you to banishment from our midst forever, but the final decision on that must rest with those assembled here today in the sight of God. It will be decided by a show of hands in a short while, but before that it is customary for those who wish to speak for or against your expulsion to do so. The meeting is now open for that purpose.'

Standish stepped forward with a solemn expression and addressed the assembly, all the while pointing an accusing finger at Thomas. 'This man took it upon himself to join our trained band when it ventured south with the laudable and Christian intention to preserve a neighbouring settlement from attack by a group of natives. When those natives turned on us most treacherously, and when it was the duty of all members of the trained band to resist, Thomas Bailey turned his back upon us, intent on saving his own neck. Not only that, but he took with him another member of that band whose strong arm could have assisted in our salvation.

'The meeting elders have decided, in their wisdom, that in so doing he was guilty of no offence, and I must of course abide by that ruling. But he *has* been found guilty of risking the lives of those who survived the initial attack by commandeering for himself our only means of retreat back to our families and friends. We must now decide whether or not such a man is deserving of continued membership of this colony under God, and it is my urging upon you that he is not. Such a man can never be trusted to act for the benefit of all, as opposed to his own selfish interests. We still find ourselves in a perilous position, with little assistance from those who first sent us here. In such a situation, we are entitled to the unswerving loyalty of every man, woman and child. There can be no toleration of self-interest such as that which Thomas Bailey has proved himself capable of, and he must be driven from our midst.'

As Standish stepped back into the body of those standing before the elders, a few sullen mutterings were audible, and it was clear that they were coming from the trained band that he claimed to command. He glared round angrily, and the mutterings ceased. Samuel Fuller stepped forward, cleared his throat nervously, and smiled in Thomas's direction.

'You all know me, and some of you have known me for as long as I have known Thomas Bailey. I first knew him back in Scrooby, a youth in the employ of Elder Brewster who stood guard outside while we conducted our prayers in Brewster's manor house. We then, as a congregation, moved to Gainsborough, and Thomas Bailey ensured that we had a roof over our heads and food on the table, all as the result of his selfless employment of the woodman's skills taught to him by his father. Neither did he behave with concern for his own safety when we made two vain attempts to leave England by ship for Holland; on both of those occasions, he stood between us and agents of the king who would have inflicted violence upon us. It was then the same Thomas Bailey who secured our safe passage to the Low Countries, risking his life with every crossing of the Channel that he made possible.

'In Holland, we still looked to Thomas Bailey for support, and we were not denied it. When we decided to join the venture out here to found a new nation under God, it was the unstinting efforts of Thomas Bailey that ensured we had huts in which to rest our heads and rear our children. Not one of you today can claim that the timbers above your heads, and the walls that keep out the winter gales, are not the fruits of his labours. Without him, and those he inspired, there would be no Colony of Plymouth, and it would be a sin before God to cast this man out. I shall be voting that we retain the company — and the services — of this most worthy of men, and I urge all those of you here today who has a love of what is right to join me in that. Thank you, Governor, that is all I have to say.'

Heavy applause followed, and Thomas found his face flushing with embarrassment. Joanna then sought permission to speak. Ordinarily women had no voice in the meetings, but the elders agreed that this grave occasion called for a different ruling. Joanna stepped forward to stand beside Thomas.

'You all know this man as my father, but the truth is that we are not related by blood,' she began. 'My birth father was a cowardly wretch in Holland who beat my mother until she fled from him, with me in her belly. She taught me to call Thomas Bailey my father, and it was the wisest decision she ever made. This man held me in his arms as an infant, fed me, clothed me, walked and played with me, and guarded me from every possible evil as we ventured here to Plymouth. I love him without question. To you he is Thomas Bailey, but to me he is "Dadda", and I will ever give thanks to God for that. Forgive me, friends, for I am overcome.'

The tears had all but choked her, and there were few dry eyes left in the room as Joanna clung to Thomas and buried her head in his chest. He gave way to tears of his own and was only vaguely aware that someone else had stepped forward and was addressing the assembly.

'I am John Ford, and this man will shortly become my father-in-law. But he might also claim to be my father, since I owe him my life. When we escaped from the native retaliation, I was wounded in the leg, and I told him to abandon me in the forest and let others see to my rescue. But he was of the belief that there would be no such deliverance, and he carried me for an entire night through perilous terrain. Without his selfless courage I would not be here today, to proudly claim him as my new father. I will go further and proclaim that if he is to be banished from our midst, then I solemnly swear before God that I shall go with him, to preserve his life in return for his preservation of mine.'

There was more applause, and it had barely died down before Thomas saw that Martha Ford was now standing in front of the meeting.

'I am Martha Ford, widow of William Ford, and mother of Martha Ford and John Ford, the brave young man who just addressed you. I came out here with my late husband, seeking a better life. For some time it seemed that was to be denied, since my husband died at sea, just before my infant daughter Martha was born. But, as we know, God moves in a mysterious way, and he has led me to the loving companionship of Thomas Bailey.

'Thomas is the strongest, most loyal, and most unassuming Christian gentleman that I have ever known, and I owe him my eternal gratitude for preserving the life of my son. He has also begun to demonstrate, to little Martha, the same dedication as a father to which Joanna Bailey testified so movingly. But there is more, if Thomas will forgive me for saying so.

'I wish to marry this man in the sight of God, here in the settlement of Plymouth that I am pleased to call my new home. If he is to be banished, then so be it, and as you have heard both John and I will go with him. But before you banish him, at least allow us to expiate a sin that we have committed. Elder Brewster, you brought these people by whom we are surrounded across the ocean in order to worship God and obey His will. We who are gathered here believe in the redemption of sin, and the sin for which Thomas and I seek redemption can only be expiated by marriage between the sinners. So expel us if you wish, but first allow us the mercy of the absolution of our sin by permitting us to marry.'

This time even some of the elders were wiping tears from their grave countenances. Governor Bradford deemed the time appropriate to call for the required show of hands.

'All those who wish to see Thomas Bailey expelled from our midst, please raise your hands.'

Three hands were raised, one of them belonging to Myles Standish. Despite the angry glares he gave to those supposedly under his command, no-one else could be intimidated into raising their hand. Bradford then called for votes against Thomas's expulsion.

The mass raising of hands that followed was audible, as almost every clothed arm rustled in unison. Martha rushed forward with a cry and flung herself on Thomas, weeping with relief.

It was an altogether lighter atmosphere the following month, as Plymouth celebrated its first ever double wedding. Joanna stood alongside John, her hand in his, while Thomas and Martha stood quietly to their left.

The service was civil in nature, but that did not prevent William Brewster leading the wedding guests in Psalm 100, a favourite of his. When it was over the happy couples moved outside, where the senior ladies of the colony had put together a wedding breakfast. There were several speeches by those who knew the newlyweds best, and they assured those listening that all concerned had made wise selections.

'I achieved four things this morning,' Thomas murmured contentedly as he kissed Martha's hand. 'I witnessed my daughter find happiness, I acquired a new son and daughter, and I am finally a married man.'

'I hope you will never have cause to regret it,' Martha said, kissing him on the lips.

'With one exception, I have never done anything without considering the consequences,' Thomas chuckled, 'and that one occasion, although it was sinful, turned out well in the end.'

'If God has indeed forgiven us,' Martha cautioned him.

Thomas smiled as he waved his arm at the settlement. 'He blessed us all in advance. We had a good harvest, the local natives are friendly, and we are finally established where we may worship Him in the manner that is most appropriate. The colony can only grow as the years pass, and we add further generations to what we have begun, armed with our faith in God.'

'Amen to that,' Martha murmured.

A NOTE TO THE READER

Dear Reader,

Thank you for taking the time to join me amidst one of history's legends. As usual it's been my pleasure to do the necessary research to explode a few myths, because the 'Pilgrim Fathers', as the founders of Plymouth Colony have become known, have been almost obscured by the legends that later admirers have woven around them. A case of too little regard for the facts, and too much desire for drama and romance.

We came away from our skeletal school history lessons with the impression that the Pilgrim Fathers were a group of religious fanatics who, having failed to impose their form of religion upon an irreligious King James I, sailed away in the *Mayflower* in a search for a land in which they could found a new nation. They — or so we were told — celebrated their success with a novel form of religious ceremony known as 'Thanksgiving', which has become almost as revered an American tradition as the Fourth of July celebrations.

There remains a hard core of truth in all that, but these settlers were mainly seeking to escape. Their origins were indeed in a village called Scrooby, in the north of Nottinghamshire, but they did not journey immediately to Southampton in order to take ship to 'the New World' in a fit of pique because the king had refused to grant recognition of their brand of worship. The king persecuted them for their Separatist observances almost as fervently as the previous monarch had persecuted covert Catholics. England might have been Protestant, along with its Scottish King, but James insisted that the Church be governed through a hierarchy of bishops and archbishops whom he could control by virtue of having appointed them. It was anathema to him to hear it declared that each church should be governed by its own congregation, and he was intent on suppressing the Brownists, or Separatists, who practised this early form of congregationalism.

The rebels of Scrooby were just such a group, and they cast wistful eyes south to Holland, where such congregations were both recognised and protected. There were other such congregations scattered around the country, and they moved initially to the small market town of Gainsborough, to be united with a similar sect that worshipped in secret, under constant threat of arrest and imprisonment. This newly combined congregation then made plans to take ship to Holland that were thwarted twice by betrayal, and they only succeeded in their eventual ambition to reach the Low Countries in small groups. The congregation then reunited, first in Amsterdam and then in Leiden.

It was only when the tide of material fortune began to flow against them in what they had intended to be their final home that their thoughts turned to the Americas. They did not originally intend to travel on the larger *Mayflower*, until the inferior vessel they had travelled in from Holland proved inadequate for the task. The fifty or so pilgrims were crammed in alongside adventurers, prospectors, ne'er-do-wells and impoverished tradesmen below decks on the *Mayflower*. Half of the number who survived the crossing went on to die of starvation, cold and fever before the end of that first winter in the Americas, and had it not been for the humanity of the local indigenous tribes, they would not have survived the second.

This gave birth to the enduring myth of the first 'Thanksgiving'. It may have been the first in the New World, but the practice was by no means unknown to the pilgrims; it was already their version of the Anglican Harvest Festival. Its significance lay in the fact that much of the food that was consumed around the table was supplied by the indigenous tribes with whom the settlers enjoyed an early trading friendship. The armed conflicts that would ultimately result in the destruction of the indigenous tribes were for the future, but they remain on record as an indictment against the cruel greed of the white men who invaded their ancestral lands.

The rest of the history of Plymouth Colony is well recorded, but it was by no means the first English settlement across the Atlantic. It was one of several, and not necessarily the most successful. Nor did these early pioneers call themselves the 'Pilgrim Fathers'; this collective title would not be adopted until a century later, when local historians lit upon a quotation from the Bible cited by William Bradford in his account of those early years. The characters of Thomas Bailey, Amy Tasker and her daughter Joanna are obviously fictitious, but the remainder are recreated from recorded history. The early Scrooby community really was led by William Brewster, and John Robinson was one of their earlier pastors. William Bradford became the second Plymouth Governor as described, and Myles Standish was indeed employed as a mercenary soldier whose duty it was to guard the early collection of huts from which modern Plymouth would eventually emerge.

I'd love to receive feedback on this novel, in the form of a review on **Amazon** or **Goodreads**. Or, of course, you can try the more personal approach on my website and my Facebook page: **DavidFieldAuthor**.

Happy reading!

David

davidfieldauthor.com

Sapere Books is an exciting new publisher of brilliant fiction and popular history.

To find out more about our latest releases and our monthly bargain books visit our website:
saperebooks.com

Printed in Great Britain
by Amazon

28452587R00116